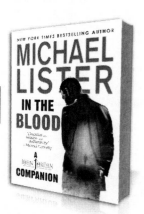

Also by Michael Lister

Inquiries should be addressed to:
Pulpwood Press
P.O. Box 35038
Panama City, FL 32412

Lister, Michael.
Blood Betrayal / Michael
Lister.
———1st ed.
p. cm.

ISBN: 978-1-888146-74-5 Paperback
ISBN: 978-1-888146-24-0 Hardcover

Edited by Aaron Bearden

Book Design and Production: Novel Design Studio
www.noveldesignstudio.com

Printed in the United States

1 3 5 7 9 10 8 6 4 2

First Edition

BLOOD BETRAYAL

A

JOHN JORDAN
MYSTERY BOOK FOURTEEN

MICHAEL LISTER

PULPWOOD PRESS
PANAMA CITY, FL

Dedication

For Fran, on the occasion of your transition into the Great Unknown. Your magnificent soul is no longer limited by the body you used up while living the most out of this life. Thank you for sharing so much of that life with me—for your kindness and support and encouragement. For your wisdom and example too.
I love you.

Thank Yous

Dawn Lister, Aaron Bearden, Tim Flanagan, Mike Harrison, Terry Lewis, D.P. Lyle

Chapter One

I am on my way to resign when I get the call.

I've spent most of the afternoon in my office inside the chapel of Gulf Correctional Institution contemplating my decision following weeks of carefully considering what I should do.

My heart is hurting and I'm still not certain I'm doing the right thing.

I've talked to my closest and most trusted intimates—Anna, Merrill, Dad, Reggie, my sponsor. I've prayed and meditated, thought and talked, written and read, but nothing I've tried has given me clarity, certainty, or peace.

For the past several months I have been working two jobs—two demanding, full-time jobs—as a chaplain at Gulf Correctional Institution and as an investigator with the Gulf County Sheriff's department. And though I love them both, I am unable to continue. I've reached a tipping point that involves the quality of my work, my health, what's best for my family, and the reality of the very fixed number of hours allotted to each day.

I'm torn because I not only find great fulfillment in doing both jobs, but I actually feel as if I've been created to do both—see each as callings, vocations, not just work, not just means to a means.

And yet I can't continue to do both—not mentally, physically, emotionally, or spiritually.

I want to. I just can't.

It's February, a month or so into a very tumultuous and surreal Donald Trump presidency. I had been wrong. I had believed there was no way our country would elect a man like him, but we did, and we're just beginning to see what that really means.

For weeks now I've gone back and forth between resigning from the department of corrections or the sheriff's department. At first I was going to remain a chaplain and just do freelance investigative work as needed—something I've done before. Then I decided to remain an investigator and just volunteer at the prison. Back and forth. Back and forth. Until I finally just picked one. And today, on the day I'm actually going to do it, I'm going with continuing to be an investigator with the sheriff's department and volunteering at the prison as I can.

In addition to all the other factors that impacted my final decision, the fact that my friend Daniel is still missing contributed mightily. As an investigator with the sheriff's department I have access and resources I wouldn't as a private citizen.

But then the call comes.

I'm actually closing my office door behind me when the phone on my desk begins ringing.

I almost don't answer it.

At first I'm not going to. I close the door and take a few steps down the hallway before turning around and digging the chapel keys from my pocket.

There are far fewer certainties in this life than most of us like to think—far, far fewer—but one absolute, unalterable certainty is that when the phone on my desk rings it's because somebody needs something. Someone has a crisis. Someone is in trouble. Someone is troubled. Someone somewhere is in need of counseling, consoling, or some other form of care-taking.

"Chaplain Jordan," I say, wondering if this will be the last time I ever say it.

"Chaplain, there's someone here to see you," the control room sergeant says. "Well, not here, but in the admin building."

"I'm on my way up to meet with the warden," I say. "Do you know what they want?"

"Said she knows you and really needs to see you."

"She give you her name?"

"Yeah, ah, Ida," she says. "Ida Williams."

I lean on my desk, a wave of painful memories and guilt washing over me.

"Chaplain? You there?"

Ida Williams knows loss like few people on the planet.

She had tasted the bitter, acidic bile of true tragedy—the kind there is no real recovery from. Her young son, Lamarcus, had been killed during the Atlanta Child Murders—and that wasn't the first or final tragedy to wound this good, kind, incredibly strong woman.

But I'm not just aware of Miss Ida's many afflictions. I share one with her.

When I was twelve years old, I had an encounter with Wayne Williams, the man eventually convicted of many of the Atlanta Child Murders. Six years later, obsessed with the case, I moved to Atlanta to attend college, take a closer look at the evidence, and see if I might be able to determine who killed the kids Wayne Williams hadn't.

When I first met Miss Ida in 1986, she was operating a daycare called Safe Haven out of the same home her son had been abducted from.

Lamarcus Williams' murder was the very first homicide investigation I ever conducted. I was young and inexperienced and it hadn't ended well—not that very many murder cases do, no matter how old or experienced the investigator.

Miss Ida is a thick, elderly black woman, though thinner since I'd seen her last, with beautiful, smooth skin, big, sad, wise eyes, and brown lips only a shade or two lighter than the rest of her.

As if she's still wearing the same uniform she always has, her hair is up in a colorful head wrap of indigo and brown and fuschia that matches her large, loose tunic dress.

I find her in the admin conference room with an attractive, athletic, stylishly dressed mid-thirties woman with short blond hair and green eyes.

The admin conference room is right off the warden's office and is where most department head meetings take place. It's also used for Employee of the

Month ceremonies—the plaque for which hangs on the wall along with pictures of the president, governor, and secretary of the department. There's little else in the room except for the large conference table surrounded by rolling office chairs, a random filing cabinet or two, a type of built-in sideboard table to hold food for the occasions when breakfast plays a role in morning meetings, and American and Florida flags that lean against each other in the front right corner.

Ida shakes her head slowly when she sees me, smiling with genuine warmth and pleasure, though the sadness in her eyes doesn't leave.

I smile back and step over and hug her.

"How are you, boy?" she asks. "You look good. Even happy."

She didn't mean it as an accusation but I felt a pang of guilt deep inside some hidden recess beneath an unseen scar.

I nod. "I'm good. It's . . . it's so good to see you. How are you?"

"Better now," she says. "It's an answer to prayer to find you here."

"I can't believe *you're* here."

"Sorry," she says, turning toward the young woman standing close to her, "this is my niece Kathryn Lewis. Kathryn, this is John Jordan, the man I've told you about."

Hearing her name reminds me of the novelist Kathryn Kennedy, who I had been involved with briefly while investigating the suspicious death of a young woman undergoing exorcism at St. Ann's Abbey. I haven't thought of her in quite a while, and I wonder how she's doing.

I extend my hand. "It's nice to meet you."

"It's an honor to meet you," she says. "Ida's told me so much about you."

I look back at Ida. "Would you like to sit down?"

She nods and the three of us take a seat at one end of the large wooden admin conference table.

"How many innocent men you think is here?" Ida asks.

"Incarcerated here at GCI?" I say. "Not nearly as many as claim to be and far more than most people realize."

You often hear people in the department of corrections and throughout the criminal justice system as a whole say that if an inmate isn't guilty of what he's charged with he's guilty of something, but it's simply not true. Our deeply flawed justice system, like everything else in the world, favors the wealthy and exploits the poor, and far, far too many actual innocent people, particularly minority men, have had their lives chewed up in the gears of the massive, grinding machine of the prison industrial complex.

She nods her head. "My nephew Qwon is one of them."

"I didn't know you had a nephew here," I say.

"Acqwon Lewis," Kathryn says.

"Kathryn's stepbrother," Ida says. "And he's as innocent as I am."

"We came to visit him today," Kathryn says, "but they won't let us see him. Aunt Ida came all the way from Atlanta."

"Did they say why?" I ask.

"Say he in lockup or lockdown or somethin' like that," Ida says.

"Would you mind goin' and checkin' on him for us?" Kathryn asks.

"*Check on him*, hell," Ida says. "Want you to do far more than that. I want you to solve his case like you did Lamarcus's and get him outta this awful place."

Chapter Two

"With no evidence," Kathryn says, "without even so much as a body, Qwon, who was eighteen at the time, was convicted of killing his seventeen-year-old girlfriend Angel Diaz."

The name Angel Diaz sounds familiar, but I don't immediately know why.

My expression must make me appear more dubious than I actually am.

"I know how it sounds," she says.

"No matter how it sounds," Ida says, "that's how it is."

"How many men you know get convicted of murder without the body of the alleged murder victim?"

"Not many," I say.

"And not just at the time," she says. "To this day."

Ida adds, "Poor girl's body never been found."

"How can you have a murder without a body?" Kathryn says.

It's possible, but I know what she means.

"They's no evidence against him 'cause he didn't kill her," Ida says. "They's no body 'cause whoever did it hid it so it'd never be found."

"That or she's not actually dead," Kathryn says. "I've always thought she might have just run away."

"I know you have, child, but . . ." Ida shakes her head and sighs. "Who knows. You may be right. All I know is whatever happened to that poor girl, Qwon didn't have nothin' to do with it."

"Exactly," Kathryn says. "Obviously, if she's not dead, Qwon didn't kill her, but even if she is, he still had nothing to do with whatever happened to her. Did you know he passed three different polygraphs at the time?"

"He did?"

"Three different polygraphs given by three different administrators at three different times," Kathryn says.

"May not be admissible in court," Ida says, "but . . . they gotta mean somethin'. State's attorney just pretended like they didn't even exist."

"That's because the investigation focused in on Qwon from the beginning," Kathryn says. "They always look at the boyfriend first, but when he's the black boyfriend of a white girl . . . they never looked at anyone else. They'll tell you they did, but they didn't. Not really."

"If they had," Ida says, "they'd'a realized her ex was the one who probably did it."

"He was obsessed with her," Kathryn says. "Lost it when she broke up with him. Why the police didn't take all the threats he made seriously I'll never know. Makes no sense that they didn't look at him a lot harder for it."

"Does too," Ida says.

"Well . . . yeah, I guess it does. His dad was a cop."

"Still is."

Kathryn shakes her head. "But . . . it sure seemed like the detectives investigating the case didn't like him and wouldn't risk their jobs for him."

"They had to make up evidence against Qwon," Ida says, "and completely ignore all the evidence that . . ."

"Exonerated him," Kathryn adds. "And that's exactly what they did. Prosecutor's fallacy."

I've heard the phrase *prosecutor's fallacy* before. It usually refers to the fallacy of statistical reasoning—assuming that the prior probability of a random match is equal to the probability of the defendant's guilt. She may or may not mean it that way but I didn't ask her. No reason to get into it now.

"Kathryn's an attorney," Ida says. "Sings like an angel. . . Could've been a professional, but changed her plans when her brother was wrongfully convicted—went to law school so she could get justice for him."

"Hasn't worked out so well," Kathryn says with a small frown and downcast demeanor. "And we've about exhausted all our options. Guess I should've spent all that time and money on finding him a better lawyer instead of trying to become one myself."

"Problem's not with you child," Ida says. "It's the injustice of the system."

Kathryn shakes her head so slightly it's almost imperceptible. "Wouldn't it be pretty to think so."

"Literate too," I say. "A literate, singing attorney."

She smiles. It's a great smile, with genuine warmth and pleasure, but as with Ida it doesn't quite reach her eyes. "Not really all that literate," she says. "Just like that particular line from that particular book."

I nod. "It's a great line. From a great book."

"It is," she says. "Never cared much for Hemingway, but that book and that line . . ."

"So," I say, "without any evidence and with no body, how'd they get a conviction?"

"A witness," Ida says.

"A friend of his testified that Qwon came to him after he killed Angel, told him what he'd done, and asked for his help destroying evidence and disposing of the body. He was convincing—earnest, remorseful, not just willing but wanting to be punished for his part in it. Jury loved him—believed him, sympathized with him, thought this poor kid put in this terrible predicament couldn't do anything for Angel at that point, but he could help his friend Acqwon and that's what he did. That's what he told them anyway. That's what they believed. You'll never believe what his name is,"

"What's that?"

"Justice."

Ida shakes her head and lets out a harsh, loud laugh. "Qwon never stood a chance."

Chapter Three

"Justice and I weren't really friends," Acqwon says. "Just more like . . . acquaintances, I guess. We were in the same grade, had some classes together, but we never hung out, never did anything together. Not that I can remember. I bought weed from him sometimes. Probably smoked with him on a few occasions, but . . ."

"Why do you think he did it?"

"I have absolutely no idea—and I've spent the last eighteen years thinking about it. That's what was so shocking about it. Well, the fact that it happened, then the fact that anyone could think I could do it, but after that . . . that anyone would believe I'd go to Justice for help burying the body. I just couldn't believe it. Imagine someone you barely know accusing you of killing someone and saying they helped you, actually became an accessory after the fact and was willing to go to prison for it. You'd be in shock, wouldn't you? You'd wonder for the rest of your life what did I ever do to this guy that he would do something like this to me. Wouldn't you? It was the most surreal experience imaginable."

Handsome and fit, Acqwon Lewis is surprisingly upbeat, energetic, and youthful. An African-American man in his mid-thirties, he looks and acts at least a decade younger. His eyes are clear and bright, his manner easy and relaxed, his smile, which he flashes often, genuine and infectious.

If he's a cold killer, he's the warmest I've ever encountered. If he's an innocent man, he's served nearly two decades of hard time and shows no signs of anger, bitterness, or frustration. Even in regards to Justice's betrayal, if that's what it is, he seems more baffled than anything else.

He's inside the claustrophobic confinement cell in what is known as the box—a building of bare six by nine cinderblock cells used for disciplinary action. It's like jail in prison. Inmates who break prison rules are removed from open population and sent to solitary confinement. With none of their property and no contact with anyone but staff and the inmate who delivers their food tray, they spend all day every day in what isn't all that much larger than a coffin.

I'm out in the hallway outside Qwon's cell, squatting down on the bare concrete floor talking to him through the open food slot in the massive metal door.

It says a lot for Qwon's mental toughness and good natured optimism that he can remain upbeat in such a setting and situation.

"Do you think *he* killed her?" I ask.

"It's hard to imagine. Really is. Maybe he did. Maybe that's why he said I did it. Would explain a lot—why he did it, how he knew things about it, but to be honest with you, I just can't see it. He really doesn't seem like the type to me. And I can't imagine he could ever get anywhere close enough to Angel to actually do it. She was tough and street smart and . . . like, real careful."

"Someone got close enough to her to do it," I say.

"Yeah, that's true. I guess they did."

"Could Justice be covering for someone else?" I ask.

"I thought of that. I guess he could. That would explain it, make sense, but . . . I can't imagine who it would be. He was a loner. Never had a girlfriend. Didn't really have any friends. Can't imagine who he'd do something like this for."

"You ever ask him?" I say.

He shakes his head. "Haven't spoken to him since the night they say I killed Angel."

"Tell me about Angel, about your relationship."

"To be honest with you, it was pretty casual. We liked each other. Had a good time. But we weren't like Romeo and Juliet or anything. I cared for her. But I wasn't like madly, passionately, deeply in love with her. Don't get me wrong, she was great. And I liked her a lot. I just wasn't like crazy about her. Truth is, we had just started dating. Plus, she was like this sort of hard, tough, take-no-shit-from-anyone kind of girl. Wasn't as if you can get really gushy over a girl like that. She won't allow it."

"Your sister and aunt said her previous boy-friend was still hung up on her."

"Oh yeah," he says, nodding, "in a big way. Eric Pulsifer. Kids called him Pussifer. He was a whiney, wimpy little punk. Guy was nuts. See . . . I would think he did it, but there's no way Justice would help him or cover for him. That, and I don't think wormy little Eric could take badass Angel. I know for a fact she whipped his ass more than once while they were together. The whole thing is just inexplicable. Only thing I know for sure is that I had nothing to do with it."

I think about what he's said.

"You mind me asking . . . why you're interested in all this?" he says.

"Ida and I go way back," I say. "Way, way back. Told her I'd look into it."

"Look into it? You mean like my case?"

I nod.

"I'm not bein' smart or anything, I swear, but . . . what could a chaplain do that all the cops, private investigators, lawyers, reporters, and my own sister couldn't? Wait. What'd you say your name was?"

"Jordan," I say. "John Jordan."

"You . . . you're the one who figured out who killed Lamarcus, aren't you?"

"Had a hand in it," I say, nodding.

"And you're a prison chaplain?"

"Among other things."

"Aunt Ida and Katie asked you to look into my case and you're going to, for real?"

I nod.

"Man . . . I'm grateful and all, I am, but . . . wish it could've been about eighteen years ago—or even five or ten. Only way I'll get any post-conviction relief now is if you find new evidence."

"Maybe we will."

"Well, if it's all the same with you I won't get my hopes up just yet. I've found a way to be at peace, even happy most of the time in here, and hope ain't a part of it."

"I understand. What is?"

"Having no expectations," he says. "Acceptance is the path to peace. My equilibrium comes from living in the present moment with no attachments, no desires, just embracing what is."

"You Buddhist?" I ask.

He smiles and lets out a little laugh. "Katieist. She writes me these long letters and we have these marathon phone conversations, and she mails me these books to read. Not sure what it is, just know that it works."

"Which is what matters most," I say. "I'm gonna see them this evening—Kathryn and your aunt. Want me to tell them anything for you?"

He smiles and nods. "Thank you. Yes. Let them know not to worry, that I'm all right, I'm good. Tell them I'm in here over something stupid I didn't even do and should be out soon. Tell them I'm sorry I couldn't get word to them to save them the trip, that I feel bad they drove over for nothing. Especially Aunt Ida from Atlanta. Tell them how much I love them and I appreciate them, they're the only ones who have stuck by me. Let them know their faith in me is justified, that I really am truly innocent, and that someday, somehow everyone will know."

I stand to leave, take a few steps then turn around and walk back where I was. "Why are you in confinement?"

"I'm on TV again. My case, I mean. Every time my case is on one of those true crime shows, on the news, or in the papers, guards—well, one guard, uses it as an excuse to lock me up. Says it's for my own protection but it's not."

"What show?" I ask. "Which officer?"

"Convicted Innocence," he says. "It looks at what they believe to be unsolved cases where an innocent person was wrongly convicted for the crime."

"And you've been on others?"

"Yeah. TV shows. Radio programs. Podcasts. Sometimes it's just like *what really happened to Angel Diaz?*" He says this last part in his best, deep broadcaster voice. "Other times it's a look at the entire case. Sometimes they say I'm innocent, others, that there's a need to find her remains and give her family closure. The lady from Convicted Innocence believes I'm innocent and is trying to get the case reopened. I doubt anything'll come of it, but it makes me feel good that somebody believes me, that somebody is trying to remind people that Angel's killer is still out there, that he got away with it."

"Who do you think did it?"

He shakes his head and lets out a long, heavy sigh. "I have no idea. It's . . . it doesn't . . . all this time later and it doesn't even seem real to me. Only thing I can think of is that she crossed paths with a killer. That walking down Beach Drive she ran into the wrong person. Nothing else makes sense. No one I know would want to kill her."

"And the officer?"

"Sergeant Payne," he says. "Troy Payne."

28

Chapter Four

"Chaplain, don't let that slick bastard pull the wool over your eyes," Troy Payne says.

He's waiting for me at the end of the hallway in confinement.

Troy Payne is ignorant and arrogant—that dangerous combination that so often goes together. Jacked up on roids and a life spent in front of mirrors in weight rooms, he's a thirty-something Neanderthal with feathered blond hair, a gold chain around his neck, and too much cologne.

"He's smooth and comes across all innocent and shit but he's a vicious rapist and killer of women."

Incarcerated since he was eighteen, Qwon has spent as much of his life inside prison as out. He's never been charged with or even accused of rape, and as far as I know, no one has ever said he killed anyone but Angel.

"Really?" I ask. "What makes you say that?"

"'Cause he is."

"He was convicted for the wrongful death of his seventeen-year-old girlfriend when he was eighteen," I say. "He's been inside ever since. How does that make him a rapist and killer of women?"

"He's already got you fooled."

With that he turns and waddles away, his thick, bowed-up body, tight and swollen, making it difficult for him to move, his arms hanging out wide at his sides in the manner of bodybuilders.

Earlier I had invited Ida and Kathryn over for dinner, and though I'm already running late, I stop by my office on my way out and do a quick search of Angel Diaz to try to figure out why her name sounds so familiar to me.

As soon as the first image appears on my screen I realize why the name is so familiar, and it has nothing to do with Acqwon Lewis or his girlfriend Angel Diaz. She just happens to have the same name as one of Florida's most notorious death penalty cases.

On December 29, 1979, three men robbed a Miami strip club called the Velvet Swing Lounge. During the commission of that crime, while everyone else was locked in the bathroom, the manager, Joseph Nagy, was shot and killed.

Angel Diaz, a twenty-eight-year-old Puerto Rican man was believed to be one of the three robbers. In 1983, his girlfriend at the time told authorities that Diaz had confided in her that he had been involved. In 1986 he was found guilty of first-degree murder, kidnapping, armed robbery, attempted robbery, and felony possession of a firearm. He was sentenced to death.

Diaz was largely convicted on the testimony of fellow Dade County inmate Ralph Gajus, who testified that Diaz confessed in his cell that he had been the one who pulled the trigger. However, Diaz spoke very little English and Gajus understood almost no Spanish, and later Gajus recanted his entire testimony, claiming he lied to get back at Diaz for not including him in an escape attempt.

Angel Diaz maintained his innocence until his death.

But none of this is why Angel Diaz and his case are so notorious that the name was familiar to me.

Angel Diaz is best known for the severity with which the state of Florida botched his lethal injection execution.

On December 13, 2006, the state of Florida's execution team pushed the IV catheter's needles straight through the veins in both his arms and into the underlying soft tissue. As a result, Diaz required two full doses of the lethal drugs, and the execution that should have only taken ten to fifteen minutes took over two to three times that.

A medical examiner said that Diaz had chemical burns on both arms, and many anti-death penalty activists claimed what was done to him amounted to torture, cruel and unusual punishment.

It was so bad, in fact, Jeb Bush, the then-governor of Florida, issued a moratorium on executions.

None of this has anything to do with Angel Diaz, the Bay High junior who went missing on January 16, 1999, or her boyfriend Acqwon Lewis, who was convicted of killing her, but I now know why her name was so familiar to me.

On the drive home, I turn on Merrick McKnight's podcast.

Merrick is a former reporter and the significant other of the Gulf County sheriff and my other boss, Reggie Summers. His true crime podcast is extremely popular—not only because he does such a good job with it, but because the first case he ever investigated on the show was solved. In the process his partner on the show went missing and the guilty party got away. At that point his show changed from *In Search of Randa Raffield* to *In Search of Daniel Davis* and eventually just became *In Search of.* Having a successful resolution to his first case but losing the suspect and his partner as a result was enough to give him the number one podcast in the world for a while, but then another case he covered, the ten-year-old unsolved mystery of a young school teacher from Ocala named Lina Patterson, was also solved and the show's popularity grew even more exponentially and took on an aura of investigative invincibility.

"Welcome to another episode of In Search of," Merrick says. "I'm your host, Merrick McKnight."

Merrick records the shows late at night now, and it sounds like it. As if an overnight DJ on an old fringe FM station, his resonant voice sounds slightly haunted and a little world-weary as though he's drinking and smoking as he does the show.

"If you've been listening to the show, you know that we're delving deep into the Stetson Ulrich case, but tonight I'm putting that one on pause for a few to circle back to talk about my old partner Daniel Davis and deal with some of the rumors about him I've heard lately. But even before I get to that I want to say directly to Daniel, 'Daniel, if somehow you're listening or in case you get to hear the show in the future, we miss you, we love you, and we're looking for you. Call us if you can. But just know that we won't stop trying to find you. Not now. Not ever. So no matter what the time or date is when you hear this, we are searching for you, brother.'"

We are all searching for Daniel, but so far every lead we've followed has led us straight down a dim, dead-end path.

"So . . . now . . . onto the rumors. Let me start by saying that I love the internet, the plethora of portals average people have to both share and receive information. It's unprecedented in the history of the world and is a powerful force for freedom around the globe. That said, it's also a sewer system of some of the most hateful, ugly, unhelpful sewage certain types of sick and soulless philistines ever came up with. One I came across today on one of the many subreddits about the case is that this is all a stunt for ratings, that Daniel isn't really missing, just hiding from the public so we can perpetrate this elaborate ruse on the true crime podcast world, that we never solved the Randa Raffield case, that we made all that up along with Daniel's disappearance to get the number one podcast on iTunes and elsewhere. Now, I know you sociopaths who write shit like this don't really care, but Daniel is an actual human being with a wife who needs him and friends and family who love and miss him. We have no idea what's happened to him or if he's even still alive."

Is Daniel dead? His abductor warned me not look for him, not to come after him if I ever wanted to see him alive again, but I began searching for him the moment I knew he was missing—and have enlisted the help of any and every one I can. We won't stop until we find him, but what will we find? The man himself, his mortal remains, or nothing at all, as in the case of Angel Diaz?

"To suggest otherwise isn't just irresponsible, it's cruel," Merrick is saying. "And I would remind you that we didn't solve the case, the Gulf and Franklin County Sheriff Departments did. Everything related to Randa and Daniel's disappearances are part of official police investigations. It's in their files. It's in the statements they've issued and the press conferences they've held. It wasn't our case. It was never our case. Did the attention we brought to it help get it solved? I truly believe so, but that's for others to say. But to suggest that we made up all of it for ratings and that our dear friend isn't really missing is as ludicrous as it is offensive. And I'm asking all of you, our sane, regular listeners to shut shit like this down when you come across it. I wouldn't want even one official looking for Daniel even a little less because he or she heard it was a hoax. Help us find Daniel. He is really, truly, actually missing and in grave danger."

Chapter Five

"Everyone liked or at least respected Angel," Kathryn says. "She wasn't a particularly warm person, but she was real—always the same, treated everyone the same. You knew where you stood with her. She came at you straight, no BS, no backbiting, nothing two-faced about her."

We have just finished dinner and are still sitting around the tall cypress table Anna's nephew built her, Anna and I on one side, Ida and Kathryn on the other. Taylor is in her room sleeping. A baby monitor sits on the table between us.

Though I gave her very short notice, Anna had made Thai shrimp, vegetables, and fried rice, and my mouth still tastes of tangy sweet chili spices.

Sam is asleep in her hospital bed in the left corner of the living room, and we are talking like we ate—as quietly as possible in an attempt not to disturb her.

Sam Michaels is a Florida Department of Law Enforcement agent I had worked with and the wife of Daniel Davis. She suffered a brain injury during a case we worked on together the previous year. When Daniel, who had been taking care of her, went missing, she moved in with us.

"I hope I'm describing her right," Kathryn says. "You know how fake some girls can be—especially in high school. She wasn't that. She was strong, tough, didn't take any shit from anybody, but she was nice—very nice, just not overly friendly or warm."

Anna nods. "I know exactly the kind of girl you mean. We would've been friends."

Kathryn nods. "Exactly. I always thought a lot of her. Never cared for most of the other girls Qwon dated, but I really liked Angel."

"We all did," Ida adds. "Whole family. Felt like maybe Qwon was growing up, making better choices—in girls and life."

We had recently replaced the old, fogged up sliding glass doors in our living room with a set of french doors—part of our ongoing process of restoring and updating this aging home piece by piece, board by board—and through it I can see the craggy cypress trees lining the lake, backlit by the low-slung moon. It's breathtakingly beautiful, and sitting here with Anna at our kitchen table with old and new friends, this place feels more like home to me than any I've ever lived in.

"You know how people will be telling a story from the past and say the world was different back then," Kathryn says. "Well, it's true in this instance. The world really was a different place. The nineties had been a pretty good, prosperous, mostly peaceful time for us, our country, and this was before 9/11. That's not an insignificant detail."

"No it's not," Anna says.

"It was also a more racist and racially charged time. I realize it still is—and always has been—especially around here, but . . . it was more so then. Believe me I know. My white mom married Acqwon's black dad—something we were looked at and treated differently for."

"How hard was that on you and Qwon?" Anna asks.

"Not too hard. We knew the problem was with the ignorant bigots and not us or our parents. Qwon and I knew each other before our parents did. We were friends, even went on a date. We introduced them. The point I was trying to make wasn't about me or Qwon or our parents."

"It's about the fact that Qwon was dating a white girl," Ida says.

She has been picking at the last of a piece of pie, but places the fork on the plate and pushes it away from her.

"Well, more to the point of thinking about what might have happened to her," Kathryn says, "it's that Angel was dating a black guy. I know she got taunts and even threats at school, but I was mostly thinking about her family and ex-boyfriend. I know they threatened her—I mean specifically related to Qwon being black."

Anna says, "With a name like Diaz, I wouldn't have thought Angel was white."

"Her mom was white and her dad was Vene-zuelan," Kathryn says. "She had dark hair, eyes, and features, but her skin . . . she looked like a white girl. Was a white girl."

"For a whole lot of people," Ida says, "they's black and everything else."

I nod.

"She vanished MLK weekend of 1999," Kathryn says. "It was a busy weekend, lots going on downtown. Maya Angelou spoke and did a reading at the Marina Civic Center on Saturday night, the sixteenth."

I nod and smile. "I was there."

Merrill and I had gone together, and had a fantastic time.

"Then you know," she says. "It was a magic night."

"Really was. Incredible positive energy buzzing through downtown."

"Exactly. Ms. Angelou's presentation was so powerful and uplifting, but it's been forever overshadowed by what happened to Angel and Qwon."

"Yeah," Ida says, "he's as much a victim in this as she is."

"Maybe far more," Kathryn says, "if she just ran away or something."

"I just don't think she did," Ida says. "Don't think she could let him sit there and suffer in prison all this time."

"Maybe she doesn't even know," Kathryn adds. "Maybe she left and never looked back. She could be in another country unaware of what her actions did to Qwon or anyone else. But if she's not, I agree. She wouldn't let Qwon . . ."

"That's the only way I could see her not coming back and making this right for Qwon."

"Yeah, that part's hard to believe. Unless . . . he did something so bad she felt he deserved it."

"What the hell could the boy have done to deserve all this?"

"Well . . ."

She doesn't say anything else, instead takes a long sip of her tea.

"Well what?" I ask.

Ida says, "You started it, child, might as well finish it."

Kathryn puts down her glass, wipes her mouth, and says, "Aunt Ida says I can trust y'all . . . I . . . I've told her this but I've never said it publicly . . . well because . . . it would just muddy the waters, but . . . if Qwon was very popular with all the girls. He didn't really do anything about it . . . except flirt a little, I guess. He was never unfaithful for anything. He didn't cheat, but . . . well, Angel was very jealous. Very. If she did just decide to run away, if she was letting him sit in prison for something he didn't do, she might be letting him because of something she thought he did—like cheating on her, which he didn't, but . . . I just think if she's out there and aware of what's going on with him . . . that could be a possible reason why she's not helping him."

"Don't matter no way," Ida says, "'cause we know who killed her."

"You do?" Anna says.

"We'll get to that," Kathryn says. "Anyway, Qwon and Angel went to the civic center for the event, then to Panama Java, a little coffee shop on Harrison at the time, then to an art exhibit at the Visual Arts Center. Several of their friends saw them, including me and Darius, my boyfriend at the time. None of us went together, but a big group of us, mostly juniors and seniors from Bay High, sort of fell in together, or at least went to a lot of the same places, so saw each other throughout the night."

"Darius?" I ask.

"Darius Turner. He was in our class too. Great guy. Haven't seen him in a long time. Everyone who saw Qwon and Angel that night gave written statements to the police that they were happy, not fighting or upset in any way. I should stop here and say that everything I'm telling you has been verified and is absolutely truthful. Qwon wasn't the only one to take a polygraph. All of us witnesses did too. Well, not all, but all the important witnesses in our little group. We all passed the polygraph with flying colors. When we say Qwon was with us, he was with us. When we say he didn't leave and couldn't have done it, it's the truth."

"It's true," Ida says. "Defense team had them all take one. Said they were telling the truth. Wasn't admissible in court any more than Qwon's was, but . . . it convinced Angel's folks and a lot of other people that Qwon is innocent."

"We were all meant to be winding up at a house party in the Cove later that night," Kathryn continues, "and so were just wandering around from place to place downtown. Everything we did was walking distance—including the house, which was on a little road off Beach Drive just over the Tarpon Dock draw bridge. After the Visual Art Center, we stopped in the Place on Grace. A friend of ours was in a band playing there that night. Until then it was like this perfect, magical night for everyone. So much fun. So many cool experiences within walking distance of each other. It's not often downtown PC has nights like that."

I nod. "I went to a lot of the same places. Probably saw y'all. Friend of mine, Merrill, and I went to Panama Java and the VAC after hearing Maya. We didn't go to the Place on Grace though. After the VAC, we walked over to the Fiesta."

"We went there after the Place and I wish to God we never had."

"Why's that?" Anna asks.

"Not because of the Fiesta or what happened there. It was like everything else that night—so much fun and like this almost mystical experience. But when we went there . . . Angel went missing. Like I said, the group that wound up sort of moving from place to place together was made up of mostly juniors and seniors, mostly seventeen- and eighteen-year-olds. But only the eighteen-year-olds could go in Fiesta. Eighteen to enter, twenty-one to drink. The seventeen-year-olds in the group decided to do different things."

"That's where they lost the poor child," Ida says, "and Qwon lost his life."

Kathryn nods. "Some stayed at the Place. Some went over to Mackenzie Park to smoke or make out. Angel, who was seventeen, decided she would go on over to the house where the party was going to be and see if she could help get things ready. She insisted that Qwon go to the Fiesta without her. He had a friend who was going to be in the drag show for the very first time that night and had promised to support him. She knew how important it was, so she wasn't about to stop him from going in."

"He wishes to God he never did, though," Ida adds. "If he could take back one decision in his entire life, it's this one."

"Thing about Angel is . . . when she said something you knew it was true. If she hadn't been happy for Qwon to go into Fiesta and her to walk on down to the party early, she would have let him know it. And as far as her walking to the house alone, just remember we're talking a very short walk in safe Panama City back in 1999, and everyone, including Qwon, thought she wasn't walking alone, that some of the other seventeen-year-olds were going to."

"Problem is who was in that group," Ida says. "Been safer if she'd been alone."

"Do you just mean her killer or are you talking about someone in particular?" I ask.

"Her ex was seen lurkin' around down there," she says. "So was the boy who railroaded Qwon."

"Who?" Anna asks.

"Eric Pulsifer and Justice Witney," I say. "Eric was Angel's ex who was still obsessed with her and

Justice was the prosecution's star witness who claimed he helped Qwon destroy the body."

"Several of us saw Qwon kiss Angel and her walk away," Kathryn says. "It's the last time we ever saw her. But we saw him the rest of the night. No way he could have killed her. No way. He was in the Fiesta, visible to all of us at one time or another. You know how the place is—Fiesta on one side, courtyard in the middle, and the Royale Lounge on the other, so everyone was going back and forth between the three, but someone saw him at all times. He went outside one time to get some more cash out of his car and grab my jacket out of mine, but only for a few minutes—and on the Harrison side, so the opposite direction of where Angel had gone. I'm telling you he didn't do it, and not just because I know him and know he couldn't, but because he didn't even have an opportunity to do it. I'll tell you something else too. We were drinking. One of the guys snuck in some booze. We weren't used to drinking. We got wasted pretty quick. Qwon, like the rest of us, was basically incapacitated. He was in no shape to do anything to anybody. He had a hard time walking and dancing. Not that it stopped us from dancing to every song. No way he killed the strong, tough, athletic Angel. Absolutely no way."

I think about that. The fact that Qwon was in an altered state cuts both ways. The vast majority of homicides are perpetrated by the inebriated or stoned.

"Were drugs involved or just alcohol?" I ask.

She nods. "Some pills were passed around. Ecstasy, I believe."

"Do you know if Qwon took any?"

"I believe he did. I'm telling you he was in no shape to do anything but love everybody."

I nod. "Okay. What happened next?"

"Later, after we left Fiesta, we all walked down Beach Drive, over Tarpon Dock bridge, and to the house for the party. When we got there and didn't see Angel, we began looking around for her. Ken and Kim, the couple throwing the party, said Angel had come and helped for a little while, but left, saying she would be back shortly. They said she may have said what she was going to do or where she was going, but . . . couldn't remember exactly. They were already pretty high. They and the few people helping set up were the last to see her alive."

Anna eases out of her chair and begins to quietly clear the table.

"Save it," I say. "I'll do it later."

She shakes her head. "I'm listening. Just gonna start on them. Y'all keep talking. I want to hear."

"One girl there said she saw a guy hanging around out on the street," Ida says. "Said she thought Angel was creeped out by him and went out to tell him to leave."

"Based on her description it could only be Eric," Kathryn says. "He was way too small to be Justice or Qwon."

"Police never really even looked at Eric in no kind of serious way," Ida says.

Kathryn starts scraping the scraps from the plates around her onto one plate, but keeps talking as she does.

"We start looking for her, not thinking anything is wrong, just trying to find her. Qwon was never by himself, not at any point during the night—none of us were. Darius and I and a few other friends helped him look for her, but stopped when we saw that her car was gone. You've got to understand something about Angel. She was the type of person who, when she got tired or ready to go, she was done. She would party like a rock star, have more energy than anyone, but when she hit the wall, she hit the wall hard. I've seen her lay down and go to sleep at a loud concert or in a booth in a busy restaurant. But most often she'd just disappear. You'd look around and she'd be gone and you knew she went home. She didn't say goodbye, didn't make a big exit or anything, just left. And that's what we thought she'd done."

She pauses and I empty the scrap plate into the trash next to the refrigerator.

It'll be easy enough to verify everything she's saying—including Angel's quirks and habits.

"It wasn't until the next morning when the police showed up at our house to question Qwon that we even knew she hadn't gone home. Her car wasn't found for like a month and she never was."

She doesn't say anything else and it's obvious she's finished telling her story.

From the sink, Anna says, "Ida, you said you knew who killed her."

"Only one that could have," she says. "One who knew so much about it and took the police to her car. The one who lied and said Qwon did it to cover up the fact that he had—Justice Witney."

Chapter Six

The moon is low and directly above Lake Julia behind our house, its pale beam shimmering on the
dark surface of the water like sunshine on the Gulf in
late afternoon.

The February night is clear and cold, and Anna
and I are in our hot tub on the back porch of our
home beneath a billion brilliant stars.

Steam rises up from the bubbling water and
from our mouths as we talk. I am leaning back on the
side of the tub, Anna sitting between my legs is leaning back on me. All but our heads and the tops of our
shoulders are submerged in the warm water.

A nearby chair holds two towels, her robe, and
both baby monitors—one for Taylor and one for Sam.

"How'd it go today?" she asks.

"What's that?"

"Resigning."

"Funny thing happened on the way to turn in
my resignation," I say with a smile she can't see, but
can probably hear.

"You didn't do it."

"I talked to Ida, Kathryn, and Acqwon instead."

She nods. "But it's not like you really wanted to
resign anyway."

"True. But I can't keep this up."

Though the truth is I'm not sure how we'll be able to afford everything—including child support for Johanna and Sam's care—if I have only one job.

"I know," she says. "It's too much on you. And I want to see you more."

"That's the main reason I'm doing it."

"But you're going to look into Qwon's case for Ida first."

"Is that okay?" I ask.

"Of course. I think he may well be innocent."

"Good possibility. Fascinating case. Can't wait to dig down deeper into it."

"I'd like to help."

"Planned on asking you to. Merrill, too, if he can."

"If what Kathryn says is true, and I have no reason to believe that it's not, he couldn't've done it, and he certainly didn't get a fair trial."

I nod.

Anna's head is leaning back on my shoulder so we feel, rather than see, each other's nods.

As usual, as we talk in the hot tub, my hands are all over her body, caressing, touching, exploring—both on and under her bathing suit. And as usual, she doesn't rebuff my wandering hands, something I'm extremely grateful for. There's no way I can be this close to her in this situation with this level of relative nudity and not touch her in the way that, out of the seven-and-a-half-billion people on the planet, only I can.

MICHAEL LISTER

"You still feel like you owe Miss Ida, don't you?" she says.

I think about it before responding, eventually nodding slowly. "Yeah, I guess I do."

"You found her son's killer," she says. "Did what no one else could or would. How can you blame yourself for who it was and what happened?"

"I don't. Not for who did it. But . . . I . . . the way it all . . . I could've . . . people died because I didn't figure things out fast enough, didn't act fast enough once I did."

She turns around to face me.

"I wish you didn't walk around with that," she says.

"I don't. But when I think of it or am reminded about it . . ."

We are quiet a long moment, beneath the silent stars and within the gurgling water.

"She was your first love, wasn't she?"

I shake my head. "Not even close."

"I really thought she was. Thought that's what made it that much more . . ."

"I was in love with you when you put the green ribbon on for the children of Atlanta," I say. "When you came in and sat on my bed beside me, asked about my encounter with Wayne Williams, and hugged me. That was at least five years before I even met Jordan. I'm one of those few, rare people who wound up with his first love."

"You're rare all right," she says, and closes the short distance between us and kisses me in a way that is both tender and passionate.

Chapter Seven

The text from Merrill comes a little after midnight. I'm lying in bed next to Anna, listening to her breathing beside me and Taylor through the monitor, while thinking about the Angel Diaz case.

When my phone lights ups and buzzes on the bedside table next to me, I turn quickly to grab it so it won't wake Anna, but when I read the message I realize I'm going to have to wake her anyway.

Rolling over to face her and touching her arm, I whisper. "Baby, sorry to wake you."

"What is it?"

"Just wanted to let you know I'm about to take a little ride with Merrill."

"Why? What's wrong?"

"Nothing. He thinks he may have a lead on Daniel. Be back as soon as I can."

"Be careful."

"Always."

"I know you have to do this, but I'm worried about you. You're not getting enough sleep."

"We'll take a long nap once we find him," I say.

"Promise?"

"Promise."

After nearly two decades with the department of corrections, Merrill Monroe, my closest friend since childhood, crossed the aisle, changed sides, switched teams. He's now a licensed private investigator who works mostly for defense attorneys and organizations like the Innocence Project. He specializes in investigating wrongful convictions—particularly those of young black men, which, as niches go, isn't exactly a narrow one.

He also does a good bit of mentoring and volunteer work and has a relatively new girlfriend, a doctor at Sacred Heart in Port St. Joe named Zaire Bell.

He's not what you'd call a man with a lot of time on his hands, but what extra time he has he spends looking for Daniel Davis. Like me, he feels responsible for Daniel's disappearance and is anxious to get him back.

Ten minutes after his text, he pulls into my driveway to pick me up in his black BMW M4.

I climb in and we take off.

The night is cold. The car is warm. Drake is on the sound system. I sink into the leather seat as if it had been designed especially to my specifications.

Left at the light. Down Highway 71. Left on 73 toward Marianna, where not too long ago Dad and I had worked a cold case that had haunted him for years.

"Couple staying in a farmhouse other side of Marianna in Campbellton," he says. "Guy matches Daniel's description. Woman could've altered her appearance. Probably did. New in town. Keep to themselves. Figured we'd ride up, knock on they door, welcome them to North Florida."

Campbellton is about as North Florida as you can get. A small farming community just a few short miles from the Alabama state line, it's the kind of micro town where newcomers would be both conspicuous and viewed suspiciously.

"Sounds good," I say, stifling a yawn.

"Take us an hour to get there," he says. "Why don't you lay back and catch a little sleep. Drake'll keep me company. Wake you when we get close."

I shake my head. "I'm good."

"Ain't gonna sleep, wanna talk about the case?"

I had asked him if he remembered us going to see Maya Angelou back in '99 and if he was familiar with the case earlier in the afternoon. He remembered the night and the case, but was also going to dig up what he could to refresh his memory about it.

"Absolutely," I say.

I've always enjoyed talking to Merrill. He's not only insightful, but he's often entertaining, slipping in and out of standard American English, affecting ebonics for his own amusement. And I don't just benefit from his insights, but from the insights he inspires me to have.

He says, "Probably won't when you hear what I got to say."

"Oh yeah?"

"Bottom line. He did it. I know the sister and Miss Ida won't want to think he did. Know for their sake you don't either, but . . . it's a pretty ironclad case."

"Kathryn says no way he could have."

"What you expect her to say?"

"Says he was with the group all night," I say.

"Sure that's what she wants to believe."

"What did the state have?" I ask. "They didn't have a body. Didn't have any physical evidence."

"A credible eyewitness. An accessory after the fact who did time for his part in it. And evidence that corroborates his testimony."

"Like what?"

"Cellphone calls and tower pings match up perfectly with what he says happened. He knew things he couldn't have if he wasn't telling the truth. And he was the one who took them to Angel's car. He knew where Qwon hid it."

I don't respond, just think about what he's saying. Not many eighteen-year-old kids had cellphones in 1999, and I wonder how both Qwon and Justice Witney did.

"I know you want him to be innocent for Ida's sake. And I know why. But I just don't see it."

"So I probably shouldn't ask for your help with it," I say.

He laughs. "Didn't say that. Not like I ain't wasted time with you before. But what you need my help with?"

"Thing is . . . I can't look into this officially. It's a closed case. Gulf County investigator looking into a Bay County investigation wouldn't go over well—with either department. Reggie wouldn't like it any more than the Bay County sheriff would."

"What happens when they find out?"

I shrug.

"You willin' to lose your job over this shit?"

"Don't want to, but I've got two."

"You really feel like you owe Ida that much?"

"I'm not asking you to work the case or spend any time on it. Just need you to make the FOIA request."

By Merrill making the Freedom of Information Act request for the files in the Angel Diaz case, I can get the case files and information I need while remaining anonymous.

"I can do that," Merrill says. "Hell, who knows. Maybe I'a take a look at 'em and decide the shit deserves a second look and help your ass solve the case."

The dilapidated old white clapboard farmhouse sits at the front of a four hundred acre farm about two miles from downtown Campbellton. A smallish, dog-trot-style floor plan with a breezeway running through the center, the entire structure slopes to the left.

It only takes a few minutes to search the place and determine no one is here—and hasn't been for a while. And whoever was here last left nothing behind.

"Seem a little suspicious not to find anything in a low rent place like this," Merrill says. "Transient, month-to-month renters in a place like this usually move out quick and leave a mess behind. Not even a single piece of trash in this bitch."

I nod. "Yeah. Be nice to talk to the owner, get more info and a better description. See if he knows where they went."

"Too late to do that tonight," he says. "I'll call him tomorrow."

"Thanks for all you're doing to find Daniel," I say.

"Just gettin' started."

Chapter Eight

The next morning, on my only day off from both jobs, I drive to Atlanta to pick up my five-year-old daughter, Johanna.

Up through Marianna, Dothan, Eufala, and Phenix City, from my door to Susan's is five and a half hours—longer on the way back with frequent stops for Johanna to snack and use the bathroom.

My daughter will get all the non-driving attention I can spare on the journey back, but on the way up it all goes to Angel Diaz and the case against Qwon.

Trapped in a car for an extended period of time is the perfect place to work on a case.

I plan to start with the *Wrongful Conviction podcast*.

While it's downloading, I think about what Merrill said and the chances that Acqwon Lewis could actually be innocent.

Merrill may be right. Qwon may be guilty, but there are far more innocent people incarcerated than any of us would like to believe.

Wrongful convictions happen for a variety of reasons, but the primary ones are eyewitness misidentifications, faulty forensics, false confessions, prosecutorial misconduct, and ineffective assistance of counsel.

The single biggest cause of wrongful conviction is eyewitness misidentification. Eyewitnesses are notoriously unreliable. Study after study shows how faulty our perceptions and memories are—and how easy our recall of information can be influenced or corrupted.

In the post-OJ, DNA, Trial of the Century, and CSI world, forensic science is not only accepted as credible and irrefutable, but is believed in with a certainty that no other element of the criminal justice system is. But many forensic testing methods are either applied with little or no scientific validation or peer review, are incorrectly carried out or interpreted, or are contaminated by a compromised process. There is also, of course, much room for confirmation bias and forensic analysts' misconduct.

Not long ago, before many high profile cases taught us differently, most of us couldn't fathom that an innocent person would confess to a crime he or she didn't commit. But false confessions are far more common than anyone realized. Actual innocent people make incriminating statements, give faulty confessions, and or even plead guilty all the time. And though there are many, many factors involved, the one thing nearly all false confessions have in common is a certain tipping point during the interrogation where making a false confession is more beneficial than maintaining the truth of innocence.

The history of criminal justice is littered with example after example of prosecutors, and even occasionally judges, taking actions to ensure a defendant is convicted even when the evidence is weak or nonexistent.

In the American judicial system, the single largest influential factor is wealth. Those who can afford a good defense team are far, far less likely to be convicted than those who cannot. Too many innocent people are sitting in prison because they were represented by a weak, ineffective attorney or an overworked, under-resourced public defender who was unable to investigate, call witnesses, hire experts, or prepare for trial.

Is Acqwon Lewis one of these? If so, who killed Angel Diaz? Is she even dead?

The *Wrongfully Convicted podcast* is hosted by a former reporter named Natasha Phillips, who had once had the top-rated talk radio show in Tampa. She is smart and smooth, assertive without ever getting overly aggressive, always prepared, and her voice sounds as if it had been especially designed by the radio gods for true crime podcasting—clear, resonate, and slightly sultry, as if a throwback to a film noir actress or radio melodrama.

Phillips made a name for herself back in the late '90s, around the time Angel went missing, by taking on the sex trafficking trade in Florida. Later, after her radio career ended because her station was sold and changed formats and she began podcasting, *Wrongfully Convicted* became the number one podcast when she worked on a case with a crime reporter for the *Ft. Lauderdale Sun-Sentinel.* Together they helped in the efforts to exonerate an innocent man who spent nearly forty years in prison for a crime he didn't commit.

There are several episodes of the *Wrongfully Convicted podcast*, but I skip ahead to the one that deals with Justice Witney and his testimony against Qwon.

"Welcome to another edition of *Wrongfully Convicted*. I'm your host Natasha Phillips, and today we're going to be talking about the state's star witness against Acqwon Lewis, the inimitable Justice Witney."

I still can't listen to a podcast without thinking of Merrick and Daniel's *In Search of* show and wondering where and how Daniel is. Did he choose to go or was he forced? Is he still alive? Will we ever find him?

"I think it's safe to say that without Justice Witney's testimony, Acqwon Lewis would not have been convicted, would not have been in prison the past eighteen years. Why did he do it? What made him confess and turn state's witness? Did he accuse Qwon to cover a crime he himself committed? Is he covering for someone else? Or is there another motive we can't see because we don't have access to all the facts? We're going to talk about all of that later, but let's begin with Justice's testimony itself. Here's what he says:"

A clip of one of Justice Witney's actual police interviews begins to play.

"I was doing what everybody else was doing—looking for Angel," Justice says.

"You're speaking of Angel Diaz, your classmate who went missing the night of January 16, 1999 in downtown Panama City," an unidentified investigator says.

The clip fades and Natasha says, "That's the voice of Roddie Andrews, the Bay County Sheriff's investigator who headed the case and took Justice's confession."

"Yes, sir," Justice says.

"You were downtown that night?"

"Yes, sir."

"Doing?"

"You know just hangin' out mostly. I's dealing at the time, so I's supplying several of the kids from my school that night."

"Supplying them with what exactly?"

"Weed mostly, but a little E and Special K, too."

"Okay, then you heard a classmate of yours had gone missing?"

"Yes, sir. Girl I hang out with sometime . . . Uma Green ran up to me and said 'Angel's missing. Everybody's looking for her."

"Ran up to you where?"

"I's walkin' down Beach Drive. Headin' to some lame-ass house party at Kim and Ken's 'cause they's good customers."

"What'd you do then?"

"Turned around and started looking for her. Everybody was walking around, calling her name. AN-GEL. AN-GEL. I joined in. I didn't think she's really like *missin'*, missin'. Just figured she was fuckin' around with Qwon somewhere or decided to go home early—

she do that sometime, just get ready to go and leave without sayin' shit to anyone. You just look around and she'd be gone."

"Then what?"

"Well, everyone was sort of lookin' along the roads, walking up and down the sidewalks . . . so I decide to check some of the darker places—alleys, vacant lots, kinda places where bad shit usually happen. I's doin' that when Qwon pull up in Angel's car and told me to get in."

"Did you?"

"Yes, sir, I did. I's like nigga did you find her? He said 'Wait 'til you see this shit.' He drove out of downtown, down Beach . . . toward like St. Andrews, but stops at one of those little pullover places where white people park to look at the bay. We get out, go around to the back of the car and he's like 'Wait for it . . . wait for it . . . look at this shit.' Then he pops the trunk and . . . and . . . Angel's dead body is laying there all folded up unnaturally and shit. Motherfucker was all like, 'No bitch gonna breakup with or blackmail me. Look at that. All these little niggas runnin' around hard with their nines and their Tupac bandanas thinkin' they street and shit. Not a one of 'em ever put a bitch down.' I was like why you showin' me this shit? 'Cause nigga, you gonna help me deal with this bitch's body.' I's like hell no I ain't. 'Hells yes you are. I know shit on you, Just. Plus your prints and hair and fibers and shit are in her car now.' Then the nigga pulls out a camera and snaps a picture of me standing there beside her dead body. 'You stirred up in this shit now,' he says. 'Question is, you wants to be stirred up to the top or not?'"

Justice Witney is a showman. Very little about the way he says things seems authentic—neither the *yes sirs* nor the street talk. His language and demeanor are part of an obvious affect. But that doesn't necessarily mean the content of what he's saying is untrue. It might. What he's saying may be as false as the way he's saying it. That's what I've got to find out.

"So that's why you agreed to help him get rid of the body?" Roddie says.

"Yes, sir. Didn't have a choice. Knew everyone would believe his little goody-goody ass over my drug-dealing one."

"Why do you think he came to you?"

"'Couple a reasons. One, I the most criminal element, street nigga he know. And two, he know my uncle owns Legacy."

"And what is Legacy?"

"Affordable direct cremation for cheap ass niggas don't want to be buried."

"Did he say that?"

"He said a lot of shit. But yeah. He was like 'We can burn her, bro. No one'll ever know.'"

"So that's what y'all did, cremated her?"

"Eventually. First, I was like if I'm gonna do this shit, I gots to be high. So we drove over to St. Andrews to one of my boys. Got hooked up."

"You got high?"

"We got fucked up. Everything after that's a little, you know, fuzzy and shit, but . . ."

"Then what'd you do?"

Justice hesitates for a moment. "Ah, let's see." The sound of papers shuffling can be heard. "Then we's headed over to Legacy and Qwon was like, I left my phone and my jacket where I killed her, we got to go get it. I's like, nigga we ridin' around in the bitches car with her dead body in the trunk and you want to go back downtown where everybody lookin' for her?"

"So you drove back downtown?"

"Part of the way, then we parked and walked the rest of it."

"Did you ask him where and how he killed her?"

"Yeah. Nigga wasn't real specific. Said he'd been looking for her and got tired. Sat his ass down on one of those benches on Beach Drive that looks out over the bay. She pull up in her car and said get in. Need to talk to you. He was like, everybody's looking for you. But he got in. Left his jacket on the bench. The phone was in it. Said he had gotten hot and took it off to take a piss. Said she drove to some dark, secluded spot over behind or beside the civic center and parked. He thought they were about to fuck, but she said she was gettin' back with her ex."

"Eric Pulsifer?"

"Yeah. Said he was like, 'What the fuck?' They started arguing and fighting. She told him he wasn't gonna make trouble for her or mess with Eric 'cause she knew too much shit on him and could turn him into the cops. Also told him she knew he'd been cheatin' on her and guess what, two can play at that.

Told him she's already fucked ol' Pulsifer while he was hangin' with the fags at the Fiesta. Think she hinted that she thought he might be gay. Said he lost it and started beating her ass. Said some shit like she taunted and mocked him. Said he hit like a girl. She was a tough bitch, promise you that. Said she started calling him names and making fun of the size of his dick. Said she thought black guys were supposed to be big, but she could never even feel his little limp dick, even when he gave her all three inches as hard as he could. He said he snapped and lost it and before he realized what he was doing, he was on top of her, his hands around her throat, chokin' her, stranglin' the shit out of her, watching the defiance, then fear, then panic, then realization in her eyes, then seein' the life go out of them. Kept sayin' over and over he was glad he did it. He'd do it again. How cool it was to see the life leave her big dark eyes. Then he threw her ass in the trunk and drove around trying to think of what to do next—and thought of my black ass and my uncle's crematorium."

"When y'all went back down to get Qwon's jacket, did y'all see anybody?"

"Lots of people. All still lookin' for Angel. Not knowin' they's lookin' at the fuckin' angel of death right there in the nigga standin' beside me. We acted like we's still lookin' for her just like they was. I remember someone said 'aren't you cold' to Qwon but can't remember who it was. We pretended to look. He got his jacket. Checked his phone. Had a lot of missed calls. Think he made a few calls. Pretended to look for

Angel some more, then someone notice her car was gone and said ah shit, bitch just went home, so they went to the party and we walked back to where we'd hid her car and drove over to Legacy."

"And cremated Angel?"

"Yes, sir. Snuck in there late that night. Did the deed."

"What did you do with her ashes?"

"Gave 'em to him. Cleaned out the crematorium. Made sure there were no teeth or bone fragments or any shit like that, gave him the ashes, and got the hell out of there. Have no idea what he did with her remains after that. Said he was gonna make sure to scatter them where no one would ever find them."

"What happened next?"

"After all this, after all I'd done for this nigga he was like, 'I'm hungry. Let's go get some chicken and waffles.' I was like, how the hell can you eat? That's some cold shit. I was like, fuck no, nigga, I ain't goin' to eat no goddamn waffles after just burnin' a bitch. He was like, 'Nigga, I own your ass now. If I say we goin' to eat, we goin' to eat. If I say you payin', you payin'.' So three o'clock in the morning, we drive up 231 to Coram's in Bayou George and I sat there and watched while that cold ass nigga ate fuckin' chicken and waffles."

"Were you still on Angel's car?"

"Oh, ah, no, sir. Sorry. Forgot that. We's on his. When we went back downtown to get his jacket, we got his car too. I drove it. I was like I ain't driving the car with the body in the back."

"So you had two cars at Legacy?"

"Yes, sir."

"And when you left Legacy?"

"He drove her car and I drove his. He went and hid her car and I followed and picked him up."

"So you can take us to Angel's car?"

"Yes, sir."

"You know where it is?"

"Yes, sir."

"And you're willing to take us there?"

"Yes, sir. I am."

"And you're willing to serve time for you part in this crime?"

"Yes, sir. I . . . I wish I hadn't let him blackmail me from the very beginnin', but I want to make it right now."

"Okay. Let's go get Angel's car."

The interview ends and after a brief, suspenseful music transition Natasha Phillips comes back on.

"So, there's Justice Witney's statement to the police—well, one of them. He made several, and it's worth noting that they changed each time, almost as if he was refining his statement, editing it. It seems to have been fairly fluid throughout the entire process, though the core of it largely remained the same. What do you think? Do you find Justice Witney a credible witness? The cops, prosecutors, and the jury certainly did. And here's the thing—well, two things. No, three. Here are the three things that make Mr. Witney such a believable witness. One, the cellphone records corroborate his testimony. Investigators were able to match pings on cell towers records with the times and locations of Justice's and Qwon's phones. When they were downtown, their phones pinged on the downtown tower. When they were at Coram's up on Highway 231, their phones pinged on the Bayou George tower. When they were in Callaway at Justice's uncle's crematorium, their phones pinged on the Callaway tower. Et cetera. To me, that's huge and convincing. Though it may not be quite as damning to Acqwon as it first seems. But we'll get into that later. For now, let's just say if you didn't have the corroborating cell phone pings, all you'd have is Justice's word against Qwon's, which means you'd have nothing. Because remember, no DNA evidence can be gathered from a crematorium. It gets so hot for so long that even if a fragment of bone or tooth remained it wouldn't be testable and according to Justice, Qwon took all of Angel's ashes and fragments and got rid of them. And even if the crematorium could be tested, which it can't, it was used for nearly an entire month after Angel's body was allegedly destroyed in it. So all the state had for corroboration are the cell phone records. Oh, and the second item on my list. Number two, Justice knew where Angel's car was. He took police to it. That's also why police, prosecutors, and ultimately the jury found Mr. Witney such a compelling witness. Think about it. Officials had been searching for Angel and her car for nearly a month. Justice told them where it was and took them to it. How could he do that if he wasn't involved? If he killed Angel, he would know where the car was, sure. But if Qwon wasn't involved then the cellphone records wouldn't match up, right? And three, the other thing that made Justice Witney such a convincing witness is that he was willing to go to prison for his part in the cover-up. It's true he got a dramatically reduced sentence for his co-operation with the state, but that he was willing to go to prison at all convinced everyone involved—or at least those who mattered most, the jury—that he was credible, that he was telling the truth."

The show breaks for a commercial and I stop for gas in Eufala.

While pumping the gas, stretching, and grabbing something to drink, I call Anna.

"How're my girls?" I ask.

"All good except missing you. Taylor says she can't wait to see her sissy, JoJo."

"I love it when we're all together," I say. "Wish it was all the time."

"Maybe one day it—"

My phone vibrates with an incoming call and she breaks up. I glance at it. It's Jerry Raffield, Randa's dad.

"Hey, Jerry's callin'," I say. "Can I—"

"Take it," she says. "Call us back when you can."

"Call you back just as soon as I finish with him. Love you."

"Love you."

I click over, as I climb back in my car and ease back into traffic.

"Hey Jerry," I say.

"John."

"How are you?"

"Still not good. Sorry to call so much, but . . ."

"Don't be. I'm glad you call me. I really am."

"I just can't get over losing her," he says. "You know."

"I know."

"And the way I lost her. The fact that she could keep so much from me for so long. I just . . . I thought we were closer, that . . . we had a better relationship than that. Can't believe I was so blind, so ignorant, so . . ."

"You're being way too hard on yourself," I say. "Randa is obviously a very special person, strong and determined in ways very few people are. She's . . . she must have this . . . vault inside her where she keeps all her secrets."

"But I'm a professional. I should have—I help unlock secrets for a living."

"I'm still working the case," I say. "A lot of people are. Followed a lead just last night."

"Anything come of it?"

"Unfortunately not, but it's just a matter of time until one does. You're a good man, Jerry. You raised an incredibly capable and resilient and brilliant daughter. Hang on to that."

"But I let her be victimized, let my little girl go through a hell like I can't even fathom and . . ."

I didn't know what to say to that.

We fall silent for a few moments.

"You have a daughter?" he asks.

"Two," I say.

"Do everything you can for them. Spend every moment you can with them. Do all you possibly can to protect them."

"I will."

"I'll let you go," he says. "Please keep me posted on all developments."

"You know I will."

"I'll let you go," he says. "I know you're expecting another call from me anytime now."

I laugh. "Take care of yourself, Jerry. Call me if you need me. I'll be in touch."

We hang up and I call Anna back, but get her voicemail.

After leaving her a message to call me back when she can, I call Kathryn Lewis.

"Did you have a cellphone back in 1999?" I ask.

"No."

"How did Qwon?"

"Saved up for it. Was really important to him. He had just gotten it a couple of weeks before Angel went missing. Ironic, isn't it? Probably wouldn't have been convicted if he didn't have it. Justice Witney had one because he was a drug dealer. His was for business. Most of the rest of us, if we had anything at all, we had pagers. My parents had one. I mean they each had one. My mom would often lend me hers when I went out on the weekends—especially since my boyfriend didn't have one. They weren't all that prevalent in our circles. Not at the time. Nothing like today."

"How did Qwon save up for one?" I ask. "What'd he do for work?"

"Lot of different things. Mostly detailed cars, but he mowed grass, raked leaves, cleaned pools. Anything he could to make money for clothes and shoes and music and so he and Angel could go out."

"Thank you," I say.

"Thank *you*. I really appreciate you lookin' into it."

"Will you still if I find out that Qwon actually did it?"

"Not as much," she says, "but yeah. I will. Besides, that's not what you're going to find out 'cause he didn't do it."

We end the call and I turn the *Wrongfully Convicted* podcast back on.

"Welcome back to the show," Natasha Phillips says. "Now . . . after the first segment you may be wondering why we're even looking into the Angel Diaz case. The evidence against Acqwon Lewis seems pretty ironclad, doesn't it? But remember the name of the show. After looking at the case and talking to several people involved, I became convinced there was at least enough evidence for the possibility that Acqwon was wrongfully convicted to reinvestigate his case on the show. So . . . with that in mind, I'm now being joined by a very special guest. When Kathryn Lewis, Acqwon's sister, first brought his case to my attention and asked me to take a closer look at it and to join her in taking up his cause, she said after you look at all the evidence, you've got to talk to Darius Turner. Well, guess what . . . we have Darius Turner on the show today. Welcome Darius."

"Thanks for having me," he says.

"So happy to have you on the show."

"My pleasure."

"Let's start with your relationship to Acqwon and the case."

"Qwon was one of my closest friends in school. We hung out a lot. I dated his sister. Knew the entire family well. They're good people. I think a lot of them. And I know for a fact Qwon couldn't have killed Angel."

"We'll get to that in a moment, but tell me more about Qwon as a person back then first. What was he like?"

"Just a really good guy. Popular. Everyone liked and respected him. He won homecoming king, was voted most friendly. He was handsome and like this star athlete, yet he was nice to everybody, truly treated everybody the same."

"I'm gonna be honest with you, Darius. He sounds too good to be true."

"I know. I knew you were gonna say that. Several other people have too. But look . . . it's true. I'm not saying Qwon couldn't be a typical teenager sometimes. And he had a weakness for the ladies. He was a horn dog. He could be a jerk. Selfish. Whatever. But it really was rare. For like ninety-nine percent of the time he was just a really good dude. Ask anyone in our class. They'll tell you. Look at our yearbook. It's all in there."

"Okay," she says, "but good dudes can kill, can't they? We hear about it all the time. I never would've suspected him. No way he could do it. He was so quiet. So nice. So . . . but then they do kill sometimes."

"Sure. No, I hear you. I'm not saying Qwon didn't kill Angel because he was a good dude. I only told you about that because you asked me to tell you about him. I'm saying he didn't kill Angel because of evidence, facts, not personality."

"What evidence? What facts?"

"It's simple. He was with or near me the entire night. He couldn't have killed Angel because he didn't have the opportunity. Was never away from us, our group, for long enough to do any of the stuff Justice testified to."

"But, Darius, let's be honest. You're his friend. His sister, his greatest advocate and defender was your girlfriend. Of course, you're going to say that he didn't do it. Of course you're going to provide him with an alibi. Do you understand what I'm saying? How would you respond to that?"

"I get it. I know what you're saying. But this is what I'd say. You don't have to take my word for it. Ask anyone who was with us that night. Several of the people in the group were more Angel's friends than Qwon's. They wouldn't lie for him. Take their word for it. Not just mine. As far as Qwon being my friend, if I thought someone killed someone, that person wouldn't be my friend anymore. Period. And as far as his sister being my girlfriend, that was eighteen years ago. And she broke up with me back then and broke my heart. And it's almost two decades later. I haven't even talked to her in all that time. So . . . I have no reason to lie."

"Okay, let's say you're not lying," she says. "That would mean that Justice Witney is, right?"

"Yes it would."

"But if that's the case, why would the cellphone records and tower pings substantiate what he alleges?"

"I have no idea. I really don't. But my guess is that you could get cell phones to lie a lot easier than a group of twenty teenagers."

"That's an interesting point, and I see what you're saying—especially throughout all eighteen years. If it was a cover-up someone would have talked by now. But both the prosecution and defense's experts testified that the cell evidence is accurate, that in your words, it's not lying."

"Then I don't know what to tell you, but I am not lying and neither are all the other witnesses from that night."

"So how late were you with Acqwon that night?" she asks. "Maybe he did it after he left—or after you did."

"We were together all night. He stayed at my house that night. We were together all evening and all night."

"Could he have snuck back out after you fell asleep?"

"No, ma'am. Neither of us did much sleeping that night. Not only couldn't he have, but if he did, if it was that much later that night, or actually that morning, then it invalidates all your cell phone evidence."

"It's not my cell phone evidence, but that's a very good point, I hadn't thought of that. It has to have happened when Justice and the cell phone evidence says it did or . . . there's no case."

I pause the show and think about what I've heard and what I know about the case so far. Still don't know a lot, still don't know nearly enough, but I do enough to wonder who's lying—Justice, the cellphone records, or Qwon and his friends?

In Phenix City, I pass by the hotel Susan and I met at back when we were first trying to reconcile. Seems like a lifetime ago now—and we had shared what seemed like a lifetime before ever reaching that point. I still feel bad for not being able to make it work. I had truly tried—more than once—but we weren't a good fit and shouldn't have tried to force it to work to begin with. I was so young when we first got together, still suffering from PTSD from the Lamarcus Williams case—though that's not what I'd have called it at the time, even if I had tried to call it something, which I had not. I liked Susan. I felt like I owed her. And at a certain point I had come to believe that making it work with her was the honorable thing to do—something that really did neither of us any favors. God save me from my own sense of honor and nobility and rigidity about what is right and wrong.

A line of Rumi's poetry comes to mind.

Out beyond ideas of right-doing and wrongdoing is field. I'll meet you there.

As long as I can remember I've had a strong, innate sense of what is right—a fixed, unwavering point I attempt to live by. I often fail to live by it or live up to it, but it's always there, a beacon in the blackest night.

I tried to do right by Susan, and though my failures relating to her are many, I believe the biggest among them wasn't the end of the relationship but how long I allowed it to go on, how hard I tried to will it to work. Of course, if I hadn't we wouldn't have Johanna, the complete and perfect success within my failure.

As if my thoughts of Susan have signaling properties sent out to her unbeknownst to me, a call from her comes through on my phone.

Susan is unpredictable. And I feel a certain small dread every time her name pops up on my phone, never knowing what kind of crisis or issue it might be.

At the moment though, my greatest concern is that she is calling to try to cancel Johanna coming to see me this weekend. And the fact that I've already driven over halfway to Atlanta to pick her up is the least of it. I just really, really want to spend time with my daughter.

"Hey," I say.

"Hey," she says, her voice surprisingly upbeat. "Where are you?"

"Almost through Phenix City."

"Well, stop."

"What?" I say, my anger rising. "Why?"

"I really felt like getting out and going for a drive," she says. "So I decided to bring our little angel part of the way. We're almost to Phenix City. We'll meet you there."

"Oh, wow. Thank you, Susan. I . . . I really appreciate you doing—"

"I should do it more often. It's such a long drive for you. Sorry I haven't done it before."

Her simple act of kindness means I'll get even more time with Johanna this weekend, and I can't help smiling, can't help appreciating this woman—her mother, my ex-wife—in a way I haven't in a while.

"Where would you like to meet?" I ask.

"You pick the place," she says. "Just make sure it has food and a bathroom."

Twenty minutes later, Susan, Johanna, and I are sitting in a booth at a small Mexican restaurant eating chips and salsa.

"This is nice," Susan says.

I nod and smile and glance from her to Johanna in the booth beside her. "Yes it is."

Surely she means the three of us sharing a meal together, because there is nothing nice about the empty restaurant. The booth and menus are sticky, the old decor around us dusty and dirty, and the Mexican music being played through the cheap speakers is tinny and too loud.

"Maybe in an alternate universe it's like this all the time," she says. "The three of us, a family, eating together every evening, doing what families do."

I'm not quite sure what to say to that. Thankfully she continues, tacking toward a slightly different point on the horizon.

"Do you think there are multiple timelines?" she says. "Multiverses?"

I start to answer, but she continues.

"Would be cool, wouldn't it? Be even cooler if you knew you were living them. Would make each life more bearable knowing you had others that just might be better."

I nod.

"How is your life in this timeline?" I ask eventually.

She shrugs. "No major complaints. Certainly like living in Atlanta again. Sorry it's so far away. I know this drive is brutal for you."

I shake my head and glance at Johanna again. "It's my pleasure."

"My life along this timeline would be better if I could meet someone and fall in love," she says. "I keep trying these ridiculous online dating sites, but . . . even with the nice guys there's just no chemistry. It's so hard to really connect with someone."

"I would think a single date, especially a first one, wouldn't give you much of an opportunity to really connect."

"True. There are second dates. Occasionally a third. It's just . . . not easy."

"No," I say. "It's not."

"Are you and Anna as happy as you seem?"

Our eyes meet, and I wonder how I can be honest without being hurtful or insensitive to how vulnerable she's being about her lack of a love life. Anna and I are hit-in-the-head happy, truly grateful to be together after so long apart. Our life together isn't without difficulty and challenge and pain, but we're happy—as happy as I've ever been—in the midst of it all.

"Of course you are," she says. "It's obvious. It was a stupid question. Can I . . . ask you a question that's . . . not so stupid?"

"What's that?"

"Is she the reason we didn't work? Were you in love with her the whole time you were with me?"

Johanna looks up from the picture she is coloring. She can hear that something has changed in her mother's voice. "What do you mean, Mommy?"

"Nothing, baby. Mommy's just being silly. You know how we get silly sometimes? That's all I'm doing. What a pretty picture. I really like that. Finish it up before our food gets here, okay?"

Johanna looks at me with her huge brown eyes and I smile and nod and try to reassure her everything is okay.

"Sorry," Susan says. "I'm feeling a little manic and my words are just . . . *blah!* . . . pouring out of me. Probably because you picked a restaurant so close to that damn hotel over there."

I follow her gaze out the window, across the street, and up the way to the hotel where we met when we were trying to reconcile, the one where we couldn't wait to get in the room and made love in the parking lot.

"Sorry," I say. "Didn't realize it was visible from here."

"Wouldn't be if it weren't at the top of that damn hill like some sort of . . . I have to see it every time I go home to see my folks. Anyway . . . it's not your . . . I'm the one who said let's meet in Phenix City. It's all good. Oh, thank Goddess. Here's our food. Let's eat."

As we eat, the atmosphere around us improves, and Johanna, who can feel it, is palpably relieved.

"Your little sister sure misses you," I say to Johanna. "Can't wait to see her big sissy JoJo. You're her favorite person on the planet. She wants to be just like you."

"I do too," Susan says.

"What are you doin' this weekend, Mommy?" Johanna asks.

"Not sure, sweetie. I have some work, but . . ."

"You work too much, Mommy."

"Think so? Well, maybe I'll take it off . . . *though* . . . if Mommy works this weekend . . . I'll have more time to spend with you next week. Would you like that? Tell you what . . . you just have a good time with your dad and little sister . . . Mommy will have a good weekend and have extra time to spend with you next week."

"Okay Mommy. Love you."

"I love *you*, sweet pea."

On the drive home, as Johanna is talking and telling me about her week, as we sing to her favorite songs, play games, make up stories, I think about Angel Diaz's parents and how, in many ways, having a child missing has to be worse than having one dead.

At some point Angel was five like my Johanna. She sang and played games and talked incessantly about everything that came into her little head. I can't even imagine losing Johanna and I won't. Won't let myself take even one step down that dark path. I can't. But what I *can* do is find Angel Diaz. Find her, find out what happened to her, and find out who's responsible. Not that any of that will make anything better. Certainly hasn't for Randa Raffield's parents so far. Didn't bring back Janet Leigh Lester—or Martin Fisher or Lamarcus Williams or Hahn Ling or Jordan Moore or Molly Thomas or little Nicole Caldwell. But I could no more not attempt to do it than I could halt the relentless march of time.

It doesn't take long for Johanna to fall asleep. When she does, I call Susan.

"You okay?" I ask.

"Will be. I'm just . . . feeling a bit . . . I don't know . . . lost."

"Sorry," I say. "Wish there was something I could do."

"Yeah, me too, but . . . we both know there's not. Listen, you don't have to drive Johanna back on Sunday. I've decided to go spend the weekend in Panama City Beach, so I'll come through and get her on my way home Sunday afternoon. I wasn't planning on it—didn't even pack any clothes, but I'll just buy a few things once I get there."

"I hope you have a relaxing, restful, and fun time over there," I say. "Since no one else knows what you're doing, would you mind texting me when you get in safe?"

"Thanks, John. I didn't want to have to tell my folks or anyone, so I appreciate it. And I'm sure it'll be like all my other weekends, but hey, I'll be alone in some place different, some place pretty. Who knows, maybe the love of my life is some widower snowbird and I'll meet him at some sad early-bird buffet. We'll have a meet-cute where we both reach for the last crab leg and look into each other's lonely eyes and . . . *bam!* Lightning bolts."

I laugh. "That's really funny. I hope it happens, but you should write it either way. Turn it into a sweet, funny romance novel."

"If I do anything with it, it'll be a screenplay. Nobody reads anymore."

"Take care of yourself," I say. "And get out and enjoy yourself. Don't just go to the buffet. Ride out to Seaside. Go to a play or concert. Wait, I think the songwriters festival is this weekend. You'd love it."

For just a moment I think about trying to introduce her to Jerry Raffield, but quickly realize it's not a good idea and not my place to do even if it were.

It's just . . . I can't stop caring about her, wanting her to be fulfilled, wanting her to have with someone what I have with Anna.

It's Anna's voice I hear next. *You can't save the world, John. People have to find their own way in their own time—and some just don't want to, don't want to do what it takes and you can't do it for them.*

"I just might do that," she says. "I'd much rather have a meet-cute with a young, hot musician than a wrinkled old snowbird."

"Be careful. Enjoy yourself. Call if you need anything."

"Kiss our angel for me. I'll call her tomorrow."

The next part of the drive home is uneventful. I talk to Anna and let her know I'll get back some three hours before we thought I would and spend the rest of the time thinking about Justice's testimony and how it contradicts what Qwon and the others have said.

And then the call comes.

It's Rachel Peterson, the first female Inspector General of the Florida Department of Corrections.

She and I had worked a few cases together when I was at Potter Correctional, but nothing since I had transferred to Gulf.

She's tough, strong, smart, and young for her position.

With no greeting or preamble she says, "What we hoped wouldn't happen is happening."

"What's that?"

"Chris has decided not to take the plea deal and testify against Randy Wayne and the others, and is instead gonna roll the dice on a jury trial of his own."

Chris Taunton, Anna's ex-husband, had confessed to several serious crimes and agreed to a plea deal for testifying against his conspirators. Rachel and I had worked on the case together—the strongest part of which was the confession I had gotten out of Chris—and had hoped he would stick with the plea deal so my involvement in his case would never be an issue his defense attorney could exploit.

"Can't say I'm surprised, but damn it, man."

"Means he has a good defense attorney who thinks he can have everything the guy who's now with his ex-wife uncovered thrown out," she says, "which is everything. All the evidence we collected at the du-plex was after the confession you got out of him. Means there is no case. He's gonna walk."

I know she's right. I know how it looks. The worst defense attorney in the world could make the case that I set up Anna's ex-husband to get rid of him. That's not what happened. Chris tried to have us killed. We survived and figured out he was behind it, and in a moment when he was feeling particularly vul-nerable I had convinced him to confess and take the deal. And it was after and because of that confession that the evidence against him was collected. Anna and I did nothing wrong. Chris committed murder and at-tempted murder. But a court case isn't about what happened. It's about what can be proved, what attor-neys can get a jury to believe. And all of that means Chris will walk.

"Anyway," Rachel says, "wanted you to hear it from me and to let you know that the state's attorney not only blames you but plans to use you as the scape-goat."

"I really appreciate you letting me know," I say.

"I'll go on record, tell anyone who'll listen that everything you did was righteous and that anyone who says otherwise is either guilty or avoiding political fallout, but . . . can't imagine anybody's gonna listen to me."

"Thank you."

"You okay?"

"Yeah. Been a long day and . . . I'm not gonna lie . . . this is some of the worst news I've received in a while—"

"Sorry."

"But mostly I hate it for Anna and Taylor."

"Let me know anything I can do," she says.

We end the call as I'm coming into town.

Anna has Johanna's bed ready and I transfer her without waking her up, and then with both girls in bed, Anna and I sit on the back patio together.

It's a dark night. No stars are visible and only the hint of a thumbnail of moon behind a bank of clouds.

Julia is peaceful, the lights of the houses and grocery store across the way reflecting on her surface looking like a coastal town seen from offshore.

We tell each other about our days.

She goes first. Besides caring for Taylor and finishing some legal work she had, she was able to delve deeper into the Angel Diaz case. "I don't want to," she says, "but I think he did it."

I nod. "He may have. Just want to be sure."

"I'll keep digging. How was Susan?"

I tell her.

"Did she let you know she arrived safely?" she asks.

I nod. "Just a few minutes ago."

"I feel so bad for her," she says.

"Me too."

"But maybe this'll be what finally motivates her to make the changes she needs to in order to have the life she wants."

"Hope so."

We are quiet a moment.

"I have some bad news," I say.

"Thanks for not leading with it. This has been nice."

"We're together," I say. "That's always nice. And compared to that, nothing else ultimately matters. We can deal with anything that comes along."

"Never doubted that," she says. "What is it?"

I tell her what Rachel Peterson told me about Chris.

"*Fuck*," she says. "*Fuck*."

"I know. I'm so sorry."

"I'm sorry for you and Taylor the most. Can't believe that asshole state's attorney is going to blame you. And I can't believe our little girl is going to have to grow up with a sorry piece of dad like that in her life."

"We'll do all we can to limit his influence and involvement. Given all he's done do you think we can get a judge to prevent him from being in her life at all?"

"Probably not, but I'm certainly gonna try. The nice thing about the court system is nothing happens fast. It's not like he'll be out tomorrow. We've got a little time to work on it. And who knows, maybe we can talk the state's attorney into proceeding with the case by telling him he can always blame you if he loses."

"That would be great," I say. "We just might be able to. I know Rachel would get onboard for that. We need to talk to TPD and FDLE and everyone else involved. Maybe we can create enough pressure that he has to do it."

Soon we are so tired and talked out we just sit there in the cool, peaceful darkness, but eventually we get up and head to bed, and the long, long day ends in the best way possible—in each other's arms with our girls not far from us sleeping safely beneath the same roof.

Chapter Nine

"Happens more than you think," the judge says. He's talking about murder cases and even convictions without a body.

He and Anna and I are sitting on a wooden bench at Lake Alice Park watching Taylor and Johanna play on the monstrous jungle gym in the huge sandbox.

It's Saturday morning, mid-February, just a couple of months before we'll be back up here at the park with the rest of our town for the Tupelo Festival.

Harlan Gibbons is a soft-spoken elderly man with wispy gray hair and ice blue eyes. Everyone in the area calls him Judge or the judge and has for as long as I can remember. Before he retired he was the longest sitting judge in Gulf County history.

"Not so often as to be common," he says, "but . . ."

When he agreed to meet with me and answer questions about murder cases without a body, I suggested the park, which is walking distance from both our homes, so the girls could play and we could enjoy the beautiful day.

It's cool but not cold. Lake Alice, the sister lake to Julia—the one just across the way that we live on— is calm, only the occasional breeze or passing ducks rippling her smooth surface. The day is bright and clear, the morning sun looms large in the sky above us and dapples the ground around us with the shadowed shapes of oak limbs.

"Lots of people still believe you can't have a crime without a body," the judge says. "Think *corpus delicti* literally means the body of the crime, but it actually refers to the body of evidence, the entirety of a case indicating a crime was committed."

Sitting beside me, Anna, who has studied and loves the law and is herself a lawyer, listens to the judge and watches our daughters, but I can tell she's still upset by the news about Chris from last night and is still ever so slightly distracted by it.

"Seems like I recall there have been over three hundred cases with convictions without a body in our country alone," he says. "Been many more than that tried. That's just the ones with a conviction. Weren't all murder. Many are manslaughter or wrongful death. But that's not an insignificant number."

"No, it's not," Anna says. "Think I read that there have been about four hundred and seventy such trials."

"They have a surprisingly high conviction rate," the judge says. "Probably because prosecutors only take the best cases to trial. They figure, I've got no body, I better have everything else. Part of the reason it's more and more common is because more and more murderers are attempting to destroy their victim's bodies, and on the other side, more and more advances in scientific techniques and sophisticated forensic procedures. Criminals, at least the non-stupid ones, are getting more and more creative. Remote, secret, deep burials, using acid or fire to obliterate the remains. Guy in Florida used alligators. Brothers in Michigan used pigs. And don't forget about the infamous wood chipper used by the man in Connecticut. Then of course there's cannibalism."

"I've only come across one case where someone was convicted of murder without a body, and the person later showed up alive," Anna says.

The judge nods. "Far as I know that's all there's been so far. Charlie Somethinganother, wasn't it?"

"Charles Hudspeth," she says. "In 1886 he was convicted and even executed for killing his lover's husband. The husband was later discovered to be alive—living in another state."

"My question for your young legal mind is," the judge says to Anna, "is one innocent defendant convicted and executed worth two-hundred and ninety-nine guilty ones getting what they deserve, or is it worth two-hundred and ninety-nine murderers getting away with it to save one innocent man?"

"Truth is if any of them kill again, then it's not just one innocent being executed, is it?"

"True."

"But . . ." she says, "our system is set up on the principle that it's far better for the guilty to go free than the innocent to be convicted, and I agree with that. Even . . . when it's my ex-husband."

I take her hand and we sit in silence for a moment.

The girls are crawling through the plastic tunnel of the jungle gym, giggling and squealing occasionally with the purity of their pleasure, Johanna being very patient and careful with her little sister.

"I remember your case," the judge says, referring to the trial of Acqwon Lewis for the murder of Angel Diaz.

I have to limit the number of people who know I'm looking into the case, but have no doubt at all that I'm safe in trusting the discretion of this wise, honorable old man.

"Followed it at the time," he says, "even talked to Judge Carr about it while it was going on. He's a friend of mine. We often ask each other's advice—or did. I thought it was a thin case at the time. Still do. Can't have charges that serious, a case that important determined by one witness. Especially a witness like him."

"What do you mean—like him?" I ask.

"Juvenile delinquent on his way to becoming a career criminal. Shifting story. So many theatrics in his statements and testimony. I would've needed more."

"The fact that the cellphone tower pings corroborated his story and that he knew where the victim's car was wasn't more enough?" Anna asks.

He shakes his head. "Not for me. Was for Judge Carr. But . . . wouldn't have been for me. I just didn't trust him. Not with so much on the line. Carr kept pointing out the cellphone evidence and the fact that he led the investigators to the car, but I don't think even that was enough for him, 'cause he kept sayin' over and over, *but Harlan he confessed.*"

"Who confessed?" I ask.

"Lewis," he says. "The defendant. Acqwon. That's what tipped it over for Judge Carr. It got thrown out. Was deemed inadmissible, but Judge Carr knew about it and listened to the recording. Without it I think he would have dismissed the case."

Chapter Ten

"You *confessed?*" I say.

"Sir?"

It's Saturday afternoon. I'm back in Confinement, squatting in the hallway in front of Qwon's cell, talking to him through the open food tray slot in the door.

From somewhere down the hall, I hear Sergeant Troy Payne laugh. It's a wicked, I-told-you-so cackle that bounces off all the hard cement and metal surfaces and reverberates through me.

I decide to lower my voice.

"Don't *sir* me," I say.

"I'm confused," he says. "Sorry. I just don't understand."

"Why didn't you tell me you confessed to killing Angel?" I say.

"Oh, that," he says, as if relieved. "I thought you knew."

"How would I know?"

"I don't know what you know and don't know about my case," he says. "I thought you knew most everything before we spoke. Thought Aunt Ida and Katie told you."

"Well, they didn't," I say.

I plan to talk to them next.

"I'm sorry," he says. "I didn't know. I'm sure they weren't intentionally hiding it from you."

"I'm not."

"You think they told you everything about my case but that?"

He makes a good point. Of course they didn't get to everything. Not even close.

"No," I say, "but I bet it's the biggest thing they left out."

He shrugs. "I really can't see either of them keeping it from you. I really can't. Can you? They're good people. You've known Ida longer than I have."

"I'm sure they planned to get around to it eventually," I say. "Would have to. And them being good people has nothing to do with the strategies they employ to try to get you out of here. But I'll talk to them about that. Why don't you tell me about killing Angel Diaz?"

"I didn't."

"Have you confessed to killing any other girls?" I ask.

He drops his head slightly. "No."

"You said you did it but you really didn't, is that it?"

"I know how it sounds, but yes, sir. That's the truth of it. I lied. They got Justice to lie against me and they got me to lie against myself."

"How'd they do that?"

"I was an eighteen-year-old kid. They held me for so long. Interrogated me all night. I was so scared, so . . . I just wanted to sleep, to see someone I knew,

my family. I was so sad at losing Angel. I was messed
up in the head. They knew what they were doing. Told
me they had all this evidence against me and this witness. DNA, cellphone, fingerprints, a witness. Said I
was going to get the electric chair. Unless . . . I just
signed my name to the paper. If I did that I could see
my family. I could leave that little room. I could eat
and drink and sleep. I don't know why I did it. I
wouldn't under normal circumstances, but . . . Let me
tell you something. Just being in here, in this cell I'm
in right now . . . It's a reminder. How much of this do
you think I can take, how much solitude, how much
deprivation, before I'd say almost anything they
wanted me to just to get out of here?"

"So all you did was sign a piece of paper?" I
say.

"Yes, sir."

"Then why is there a recording of you confess-
ing?"

"There's not. I mean, they may have had me . . .
maybe they made me read what they wrote on the paper, but . . . I don't really remember doing that. I was
so out of it, so . . . and for some reason none of this
was in my trial. Haven't thought about it in a long,
long time."

I nod.

"I swear I wasn't trying to deceive you," he
says. "And I know they weren't either."

"We'll see about that."

"John, take a breath and slow down a bit," Anna says.

Back in my office, about to call Ida, I call Anna first.

"I know what it looks like, but give them a chance to explain before you take their heads off."

I sit back in my chair and take a deep breath.

She's right. I can feel the anger and tension in my body. I'm worked up—a state that doesn't serve me well.

I exhale slowly.

After a few moments, I can feel my heart rate decreasing, the tension in my body easing, the anger slowly dissipating.

"Thanks," I say.

"I understand how you feel," she says. "And if they lied to you and or if he's guilty and you want to drop the case that's fine. But give them a chance to respond first and stay calm even if you walk."

"You're right. Appreciate the reminder. I went from zero to sixty as soon as the judge said *confession*."

"It's understandable."

I don't respond, just continue to relax, focus on my breathing.

"You good?" she says.

"I am. Thanks. Thank you for—"

"No need to thank me. Call them and see what they say and call me back. But no matter what . . . don't forget how often false confessions occur. Just keep it in mind. Walk away from the case today if you want to. Fine by me. Just don't forget."

"I won't. Call you back in a few. And thanks again."

When I'm off the phone with Anna, I get another outside line from the control room and call Ida.

"You already solved it, ain't you, boy?" she says.

"No, ma'am. Just getting started. Don't even have all the information yet."

"Oh. Well, that's okay."

"Speaking of all the information," I say, "why didn't y'all tell me Qwon confessed?"

There's a long silence. Eventually she says, "Let me let you speak to Kathryn."

"Hey, John," Kathryn says in another moment. "How's it going?"

"Not well," I say.

"What's wrong? What's happened?"

"I just found out that Qwon confessed to killing Angel and that you and Ida kept it from me."

"Oh."

That's all she says for a moment, and we fall into more silence.

"Ida wanted to," she says finally. "She wanted to go ahead and get it out of the way, but . . . I wanted you to look into the case some first. I'm . . . it was a calculation on my part. Ida was against it, but went along with it since I was the one doin' most of the talking. It's my fault. I'm sorry. I should have told you sooner."

"What else haven't you told me?" I ask.

"So much," she says, "but only because we haven't gotten to it yet. I was going to tell you, this weekend in fact, when I gave you the copies of the case files."

"You made me copies of—"

"Everything," she says. "Everything we have. All the defense files, all the documents I've managed to get from my many FOIA requests. You'll have everything we have. Everything. Not holding anything back."

I don't respond right away.

She says, "Please don't quit on Qwon because of something stupid I did. He made a false confession. It happens all the time. He was a scared black kid. He hadn't slept. Hadn't eaten. Hadn't had anything to drink. He was bullied and manipulated and coerced. Every civil right he had was violated. They threatened him with a loaded gun. Played Russian roulette on his forehead. Terrorized him. Tortured him. There's a reason it wasn't allowed in the trial. Think about it. I get that you're mad at me. You have every right to be. But don't blame Ida and don't take it out on Qwon. Just ask yourself . . . what do you put more stock in, the coerced confession of a kid being tortured or three different polygraphs given by three different administrators at three different times?"

Chapter Eleven

As usual I use some of my much accrued comp time to take off early so I can maximize my time with Johanna, and she and Taylor and Anna and I spend Saturday evening at the Dead Lakes Campground.

While Taylor and Joanna play on the swings and playground equipment, Anna and I grill hotdogs and talk about false confessions.

Previously a state park, the campground is not managed by the county. Beneath tall, old thick-bodied pines, the campground is a bowl that gently slopes down toward a small lake. Nature trails cut through the woods and edge of the swamp. On one side RV hookups and tent sites surround a small cinderblock building of restrooms and showers, while on the other picnic pavilions and built-in grills are situated near the kids' playground area.

It's a clear, cool evening growing colder with the sinking of the sun. Both girls have on coats, but are running and playing so much they are actually sweating a little.

The hotdogs on the grill smell better than they really are, but they're the girls' favorite and are befitting an evening picnic in a North Florida pine forest.

As a defense attorney, Anna knows a thing or three about false confessions and learned even more during her research this afternoon.

"I know you know they happen," she says, "but you'd be shocked and disturbed at just how pervasive they really are. There have been something like three hundred and twenty post-conviction DNA exonerations in the US. Of those, thirty percent included incriminating statements, false confessions, and guilty pleas. Thirty percent."

"And that's just the ones we know of," I say. "Wonder how high the actual number really is?"

"Exactly. Scary thing is . . . most were in homicide cases and many of the innocent people did time on death row."

Nearly everyone says there's no way they'd confess to a crime they didn't commit, no matter what. But nearly everyone has a breaking point, and the circumstances under which false confessions are obtained are exceptionally good at finding it.

There are many reasons for false confessions, and the more vulnerable the person being interviewed, the more likely they are to occur. Juveniles and those with a low IQ or mental handicap are particularly susceptible to the common factors like duress, coercion, fear of or actual violence, and ignorance of the law. Other factors include intoxication, diminished capacity, threat of a harsher sentence, and something as simple as a misunderstanding of the situation.

The interrogation techniques of law enforcement officers play a particularly large part in false confessions. The impact of psychologically breaking someone down over extended periods of time—sometime as much as twenty-four hours or more—cannot be overstated.

At a certain point interviewees will do just about anything to end the interview and get out of the small room they've been trapped in for so long under such duress.

One of the primary reasons innocent people give false confessions is they believe the investigation will prove their innocence and they'll be vindicated, but of course, ironically in most cases, their confession is the very thing that brings the investigation to an end.

As Anna prepares our picnic, grilling the hotdogs and warming the buns, pulling out containers of onions and relish, condiments and chips, I'm keeping an eye on the girls, who are edging farther and farther away from us toward the lake.

"Johanna, Taylor," I say. "Come back up this way."

Taking her solemn duties as big sister seriously, Johanna takes Taylor by the hand and they walk back toward us.

"You better keep a very close eye on them," Anna says in mock seriousness.

I smile. A recent headline in Backpack Verse that had come to locals' attention was: A Kindly Old Man Swears Bigfoot Lurks at this Florida Campground. The story beneath the headline says a seventy-five-year-old from Rochester Hills, Michigan, an avid bird lover whose name was changed for privacy, claims he saw Bigfoot at the Dead Lakes Recreational Campground in Wewahitchka, Florida.

In the article, the elderly man stated, "I was walking near the campgrounds that surround the lakes in the area, peering into the trees, listening for telltale bird calls. I must have been out there for about a half hour, maybe more, when I saw something huge pass between the small gap between two massive willow trees, not far from the water's edge. Whatever it was moved fast, but even so I could tell that it was massive in size, and covered in dense, brown hair."

I've heard many locals say they know what it was—a certain wooly member of a notoriously unwashed family in town, especially because the elderly gentleman from Rochester Hills, Michigan went on to say, "The closer I got, I realized there was a pungent odor lingering in the air. It was awful, truth be told. It reminded me of some vile combination of a wet, dirty dog and the smell of rotten meat. I fought the urge to gag."

"I'm surprised you let us bring them here at all," I say. "Considering the risk involved."

She glances over at the girls, then at me, gives me a sweet little smile, then returns to her preparations.

"Given what you know about the prevalence of false confessions," she says, "why did you react the way you did when you found out Qwon had confessed?"

"My reaction or overreaction wasn't as much about his confession as them lying to me," I say.

She nods. "I certainly understand that. But you can see why they did it. And in the same situation you might have done the same."

I nod and smile. "I just might have."

"From what I've seen and heard of Qwon's case, I'd say he's a perfect candidate for a false confession—a black kid with no lawyer and no guardian under interrogation for nearly twenty-four hours."

"You're probably right," I say. "And if we survive this visit to Sasquatch's hunting ground, we'll try to find out for sure."

Chapter Twelve

We are putting the girls to bed when Ida and Kathryn show up to bring the case file.

"Come on in," I say.

"We can just leave these with you," Kathryn says.

"No. Come in. I'd like to talk to y'all some more and we're almost done with the bedtime rituals. Have a seat in the living room and give us just a few more minutes. Would you like something to drink?"

When we finish with the girls, we join Ida and Kathryn in the living room, baby monitor in hand.

"Y'all are such good parents," Kathryn says.

"Make such a sweet little family," Ida adds.

"I really regret not having kids," Kathryn says. "Don't regret much, but I really regret that."

"Dedicated near 'bout her whole life to finding justice for Qwon and Angel," Ida says.

"Lot of good it's done him," Kathryn says, adding as she looks at me, "Sorry again I didn't mention his confession. I have no excuse."

"I understand," I say.

Anna sits with them while I fix drinks for us—wine for Anna and Kathryn, tea for me and Ida.

I rejoin them in the living room, pass out the drinks, and take a seat by Anna on the dual reclining love seat across from Kathryn and Ida on the couch.

After a few moments of catching up and small talk, Kathryn hands me the thick file folder that's been sitting on the coffee table in front of her.

"This isn't everything," she says, "but it's everything we have. I know for a fact that the cops didn't turn over everything—all their notes and photographs and everything—and that the prosecution committed several Brady violations by failing to disclose everything they had."

I take it and weigh its heft. "May not be everything but it feels like a lot."

"It's proof of Qwon's innocence and maybe Justice's guilt."

"Any idea how the cops got onto Justice to begin with?" I ask.

She nods. "They got Qwon's cellphone records. Saw calls to Jessica. Talk to Jessica. Jessica led them to Justice."

"Jessica?"

"Sorry. Jessica Poole. She's an interesting player in all this. Supposedly she was just a friend of Justice's because he had a girlfriend, but . . . they seem way too close and she did way too much for him for there not to be more to them than that."

Ida says, "She probably helped him kill Angel and destroy the evidence. If she didn't . . . she covered for him to protect their drug operation and other criminal activities."

Kathryn nods. "I agree. Unfortunately, we don't know a lot about her and didn't get to hear much from her in the investigation or the trial. When the police asked to interview her, she showed up with her parents and an attorney and said very little. Then she was just gone. She testified that Justice told her that Qwon killed Angel, and they asked for her help in destroying the clothes he was wearing when he helped Qwon cremate the body, and to help him think everything through to make sure he didn't forget anything incriminating him. She said this happened on the Sunday morning following Angel's disappearance."

"Think about that," Ida says. "She actually testifies to bein' a accessory after the fact and not saying anything for nearly a month, but she's only interviewed the one time and testified during the trial. No charges were ever brought against her and she was never considered a suspect. I think Justice killed Angel and Jessica helped or helped him cover it up, or Jessica killed her and Justice helped cover it up, or they did it together, but . . . she ain't even looked at seriously."

"It's obvious they had already narrowed in on Qwon," Kathryn says. "Hell, it was his phone records that led them to her and ultimately Justice. All they were looking for at that point was evidence to prove the theory they already had—the only theory. The angry young black man Qwon killed his white girlfriend. They had blinders on to any and everything else that contradicted that."

I nod. "Happens a lot. It's easy to do. You have to keep reminding yourself to keep an open mind, that all facts matter, that all evidence is valuable— especially if it contradicts your theory or main line of inquiry. The thing is, most cases are so straight forward. Most of the time there's very little doubt who committed the crime, very little that is actually in question. Those are the ones that make up all the statistics. The boyfriend did it. Of course the boyfriend did it. It's the boyfriend in the vast majority of cases. So when it's not the boyfriend, when it cuts against the statistics, when it's the rare exception that proves the rule, even good, sound investigators can be lulled into statistical compliancy."

"That's a very charitable way to look at it," Kathryn says.

I shrug. "Maybe it is. But bad cops who intentionally do wrong are very rare."

"That may be," Ida says, "but whether they bad and intentionally doin' wrong or sloppy or lazy and blind to what's out of the ordinary . . . comes to the same thing for the poor soul like Qwon whose life is stolen from them."

I nod. "Yes it does. There's no difference for them."

"So how can you defend them?" Kathryn says.

"I wasn't."

"But—"

"Think about how many lawyers do things that adversely affect their clients. I'm sure you have done it more than you'd like. How many of y'all do it on purpose?"

She smiles then frowns and nods. "I see what you're saying."

"If Justice killed Angel or helped Jessica do it, it makes sense that his cellphone records would match his testimony, but why would Qwon's?"

"I truly can't answer that," Kathryn says. "If I could, Qwon probably wouldn't be in prison right now, but I know that he couldn't have done it, because like the rest of our group, I saw him when he was supposed to be doing it. And remember not only did he pass three different lie detector tests, but everyone in our group did too."

"Y'all were tested too?" Anna says.

Kathryn nods. "In all this time, the only thing I've been able to come up with is coincidence. Maybe it was just an unlucky coincidence that they matched."

"That would make Qwon one of the unluckiest people to ever live," Anna says.

"Maybe he is," Ida says. "Maybe he is. Somebody gotta be."

Chapter Thirteen

"I'm going back to Atlanta tomorrow," Ida says, "so I'm really glad we doin' this."

This that we're doing is having a drink at the 22 Bar.

"Me too," I say.

The four of us are seated at one of the small round tables between the bar and the stage sipping on our drinks.

We're here because Anna, sensing all four of us could use some fun and Ida and I could benefit from more time together in a relaxed setting, suggested it after checking to see if our babysitter was available.

"I'm gonna miss you," Kathryn says.

"I'a be back when they let that boy up out of confinement and we can actually visit him."

"Maybe we'll be closer to getting him out by then," Kathryn says.

Anna looks at me and smiles. Kathryn sees her.

"I know it won't happen that fast," Kathryn adds, "but . . . I'm just really encouraged y'all are helpin' us with it."

"We're happy to be helping," Anna says.

The bar, which will always be the 22 bar or simply 22 to us, is actually now the Saltshaker Lounge. Under new ownership and management, it has been remodeled and is one of the nicest and best roadside bars I've ever been in—and my favorite since the Fiesta in downtown Panama City closed.

Nearly every weekend 22 now has entertainment of some sort, mostly the live music of bar bands, but occasionally, like tonight, karaoke, which means we get to hear Kathryn sing.

"You picked out a song yet?" I ask Kathryn.

"We just got here."

"Yeah," Anna says, "but if you sing as good as Miss Ida says, we want to hear you a few times."

"Do you take requests?" I ask.

"What song is it you want to hear?" she asks in her best Ronnie Van Zant.

"One of his favorites is *Wrecking Ball* by Emmylou Harris," Anna says.

"Never seen a karaoke version of that," she says, "but it shows great taste."

"Anything at all Jann Arden," I say.

She nods her approval. "But I doubt they'll have anything."

"You're probably right," I say.

"So what're you gonna do?" Anna asks.

"Give me a minute," she says, and begins to look around the bar—both at the people and the decor. "I'll come up with something that'll fit this place. Something . . . classic and . . . country."

"This is nice," I say to Anna. "Thanks for suggesting it."

"I've got it," Kathryn says, jumping up from her seat and heading toward the stage.

After a short discussion with the Karaoke DJ, she takes the stage and removes the mic from the stand.

"I want to dedicate this to my new favorite couple," she says, "John and Anna."

All the regulars who know us look over and clap, a few of the women saying, "That's so sweet."

As soon as it starts, I can't help but smile. She did it. She picked the perfect song.

Standing, I reach out and take Anna's hand. "May I?"

We're the first couple on the dance floor, but in no time at all we're surrounded by other couples.

"Wow," Anna says. "She can really sing."

"She's got some pipes," I say, and pull her even closer to me. "Have I mentioned how much I love dancing with you?"

She smiles and nods. "A time or two."

"At the risk of being redundant, let me just say I *love* dancing with you."

"I love how sweet you are to me," she says, and kisses me.

The perfect song Kathryn selected, the one we're dancing to right now—along with nearly every other couple in the bar—is *I Will Always Love You*, and she performs it with the sweetness and sincerity of Dolly and the quality and range of Whitney, closing her eyes as she does.

When she finishes she receives the most enthusiastic ovation I've ever witnessed out here, and as she sits her eyes are moist.

"That was incredible," Anna says.

"Told y'all the girl could sing, didn't I?" Ida says.

"Are you okay?" I ask Kathryn.

She nods. "Just a little emotional. It's always there, just under the surface. Comes out if I sing the right song."

"It was certainly that," Anna says. "Great choice. And thanks for dedicating it to us. So sweet."

She nods and gives her a small smile, but her eyes are sad.

"You sure you're okay?" Anna asks.

She nods again. "Just feel a little guilty. It's hard to ever really relax or enjoy myself knowing Qwon is locked in a box."

Ida nods. "Know what you mean," she says. "I get it. I truly do, but . . . you got to live while you're working on freeing him. Got to. He would. And he'd want you to. Trust me. I struggle with the same feelings about my little Lamarcus."

"You're right. I know you are. I'm not usually this . . . maudlin. I think it's . . . I honestly think it's because for the first time I . . . I'm allowing myself to be, to feel . . . a little hope."

"Speaking of my boy," Ida says, looking at me. "It's time you let all that go. No tellin' how many lives you saved by what you did. You didn't cost me or anybody else anything. You freed us. Helped us when nobody else would. I owe you more than I can ever repay, so I better not hear anything about you feelin' guilty or sad or owin' anything where I'm concerned, you hear? Anna's gonna let me know, aren't you sugar?"

"I am," Anna says.

"That bad business on Memorial Drive," Ida says. "Out in Conyers. You . . . you . . . what you did . . . We all owe you. You don't owe me or anybody else in Atlanta nothin'."

"If you really think you owe me," I say, "you can repay it all right now."

"Name it, boy."

"Dance with me."

She smiles. "I'd be honored to, son." She then looks over at Kathryn. "Sing somethin' good we can dance to."

"I know just the thing."

A few moments later, Ida Williams and I are dancing to Kathryn's inspired version of Louis Armstrong's *What a Wonderful World*, in Wewahitchka over thirty years after we met in Atlanta. Wayne Williams is still alive. Lamarcus and all the other child victims of Atlanta are still dead. Somehow we're still here. And in spite of it all it really is a wonderful world, a wonderful, beautiful life—even more so now that she has lifted some of the unseen burden of guilt and regret I've borne all this time. There's still loss and pain and always will be, but even that has been eased a bit, too.

"Listen to me, boy," she says. "Acqwon ain't your responsibility. You work it, don't work it, don't matter. Solve it, don't solve it, don't matter. Understand?"

I nod.

"I mean it. I asked a lot of you back when you's a kid. Didn't realize how much at the time—how much I was asking or how much a kid you was. Didn't act like a kid, that's for sure. Never intended to ask you for anything again. Never figured we'd cross paths again, 'specially not in some tiny town in the middle of nowhere Florida, so when I saw you, saw that you's the chaplain where Qwon was, I thought it was a sign, an answer to my prayers. Didn't stop to think about what I was askin' of you again. Guess who ain't changed in thirty years? Thing is . . . you need to know, you don't have to look into it any further, but if you do and you find out that somehow Qwon really did it, it's okay. It's all okay. Everything is okay. Okay?"

I nod. "Okay."

She smiles. It's a great smile. And this time a hint of it reaches her eyes.

"I understand it's okay if I don't investigate the case, but if it's okay with you I'm going to. I'm going to find out who killed Angel and why—even if it's Qwon. But especially if it's not. If he didn't do it, I'm gonna find who has let him sit in prison his entire adult life and see about getting them to swap places with him."

Chapter Fourteen

The next morning, I drive to Panama City to meet with Qwon and Angel's parents. On my way I take Johanna to meet Susan.

"How was your weekend?" I ask.

"Best I've had in a long time," she says.

Her appearance corroborates her statement. She looks far more relaxed and rested, her mood is lighter, her eyes brighter, her countenance happier, not as harsh and hard.

"I wound up going to the songwriters festival," she adds. "It was incredible. Heard some great music, made some new friends, met someone."

She is wearing a new sundress and sandals and looks like she's on vacation.

"That's great," I say. "I'm so glad it was so good."

Since she's taking Highway 231 home, we meet at Coram's in Bayou George for breakfast—the same diner Justice Witney claims he and Qwon came to after they cremated Angel's body.

"How was this little angel's weekend?" Susan asks, looking from me to Johanna, who sits beside me in the booth. "Did you have a good time, honey?"

Johanna nods. "Yes, ma'am."

"What all'd you do?"

"Played . . . and cooked . . . and painted . . . and colored . . . and went camping."

"Camping?" Susan asks.

I smile. "We had a picnic at the campground."

"Sounds like we all had a good weekend," she says.

I nod.

As Johanna eats her pancakes, Susan and I mostly pick at our food.

"I've been a bit lost lately," Susan says. "Nothin' . . . major . . . just sad and out of sorts. I really needed to get away and regain some perspective. This weekend helped me do that. Life is . . . so, so short. I really haven't been living, just . . . sort of surviving. And I don't want to live like that. Thing is . . . and don't get your hopes up too much, 'cause it'd take a lot of doin' . . . but . . . I miss Florida. Like the pace and size and lifestyle here. But I've been limiting myself to Tallahassee and, well, I don't want to live in the same town as my parents. Anyway, I'm gonna look into maybe relocating to 30A or Panama City Beach. Like I say don't get your hopes up."

"How could I not?" I say. "That would be . . . so great."

I hope this isn't just because of meeting someone this weekend or the false sense of utopian feelings a visit to a great place can give you, but no matter the reason, the thought of having Johanna closer is causing my heart to do backflips and cartwheels.

"Anything I can do to help or . . . anything, just let me know," I say.

"I love Atlanta," she says. "I do, but . . . there's just something about . . . this area that . . ."

"It's home," I say.

Her eyes and mouth narrow and she nods slowly, contemplatively. "Yes it is. Always will be. And it would make a better home for our little pancake-eating angel than where we are now. It's safer . . ."

I know she's right, but given where we are and what she calls our daughter, I can't help but think of Angel Diaz and what happened to her—or Justin Menge and what Susan's own father had done to him. But she's right. It is safer and the thought of having Johanna closer has energy jangling through my body.

"I know 30A would be astronomical," Susan says, "but don't worry. I know you can't possibly pay any more child support than you already are. The thing is . . . my Aunt Margaret is dying and she's leaving everything to me, which is . . . will be quite a bit, so . . ."

At one time I was closer to Margaret than I was Susan. For a dark, difficult time in my life, Margaret had been the bartender who heard my confessions and kept me anesthetized. She had also been the one to set me up with Susan. She stopped speaking to me after our first divorce. After our second I was dead to her.

"I'm so sorry to hear that," I say. "So sorry. I've missed Margaret for so long now. Seems like I've already mourned the loss of her a long time ago, but . . . this . . ."

"I know. Thank you."

"She won't want it," I say, "but please give her my love. And let me know if I can do anything for you."

Chapter Fifteen

After getting Susan and Johanna on the road, I drive back into town, down 23rd Street to Airport Road, to the Unitarian Universalist Fellowship of Bay County.

Sunday in the South means church for a huge swath of the population. Ironically, it has never really meant that for me. I say ironically because as a chaplain, a spiritual person and student of religion, I've never been a churchgoer or had much use for organized religion. But that's just another way in which I'm out of step with the culture I'm surrounded by—the culture of God, Guns, and Guts, of Chic-Fil-A being closed on what the Baptist founder of the company considers the Sabbath, of church being the primary social outlet, organizer, and moral and political center.

Both Acqwon and Angel's parents attend UU and have agreed to meet me here following their service.

UU comes from the historical affirmation of the unity of God (Unitarian) and the belief in the universal salvation of all souls (Universalist). It's an open and open-minded group of unity within diversity which affirms the supreme worth of all persons. As a religion, it is bound by neither creed nor dogma, and attempts to honor and celebrate the right of individual thought, joined in shared concern and respect for everyone as they seek their own spiritual path wherever it may lead.

The UU of Bay County meets in a small converted house on a beautiful wooded lot with a pond not far from the old Panama City airport.

In the Deep Red State Conservative Republican South, a liberal religion like UU is going to inevitably be small—smaller even than the popup storefront fringe Pentecostal churches that dot the strip mall landscape and, in an area like this, aren't actually fringe at all.

The five of us—me, Henry and Mary Elizabeth Lewis, and Buck and Kay Diaz—sit at a wooden picnic table between the small house church and the small pond beneath the shade of oak and pine trees.

The couples are dressed casually and seem very comfortable with themselves and each other.

"I'm Kathryn's mom and Qwon's stepmom," Mary Elizabeth says. "This is my husband and Qwon's father, Henry."

I shake hands with them.

Henry Aaron Lewis is a tall, thick black man with huge hands and an implacable face. His wife, Mary Elizabeth, is an attractive older white woman with long gray-blond hair and kind blue eyes.

"We're Angel's folks," Buck Diaz says. "I'm Buck and this is my wife Kay."

Buck has dark hair going gray, a dark orangish complexion and mustache. His wife, Kay, has pale white skin, green eyes, and bottle black hair.

The four broken but resilient people appear to be in their late fifties to mid sixties with Kay being the youngest among them.

"We're meeting with you together," Kay says, "to present a united front. We, all four of us, believe that Qwon is innocent and that whatever really happened to our daughter and whoever really did it is unknown."

I nod.

"Kathryn says you're our best hope of finding that out," Mary Elizabeth says.

"A lot of smart people are working on it," I say. "We're all gonna do all we can."

"My son wouldn't kill anyone," Henry says, "and he's never hurt Angel in any way whatsoever."

"We believe that too," Buck says. "He was a very fine boy and now he's a good man."

"We never believed it was him," Kay adds, "not for a second. Even before he passed all the polygraphs and we learned what a bad guy the witness against him was. Just never did."

"And we appreciate that more than you'll ever know," Mary Elizabeth says.

"We know that sorry ass Justice Witney is lying," Henry says. "We just hoping somebody will be able to finally be able to tell us why the cellphone evidence lines up with what his lying ass said."

"We get why he knew where the car was," Kay says. "Only one explanation. He was involved, but the cellphone evidence . . . that's more . . . problematic."

"I heard recently of another case," Mary Elizabeth says, "where all the cellphone evidence was thrown out because it was no good. Think it was outgoing calls are unreliable, only incoming calls can be used to determine a location. Something like that. Maybe that's what happened here."

"We'll certainly look into that," I say.

"You should also look into all the evidence the police ignored or conveniently lost," Kay says. "They took Angel's computer, but we never heard of anything they found on it that might be helpful. They never really properly processed her car or its contents. Found fingerprints that didn't match Qwon or Angel, but never found out who they did belong to."

"Since she went missing from downtown," Buck says, "the Panama City police began the investigation, but since her car was found out in the county, the sheriff's department took over and . . ."

"Evidence was lost," Henry says. "Sheriff's department says they never received certain things like Angel's computer or all the items listed on the contents log from the car."

"Was it sloppy police work?" Buck says. "Or were the cops covering up for the son of one of their own?"

"Eric Pulsifer?" I say.

He nods. "His dad was a PCPD officer at the time. He could have destroyed evidence, called in favors, or just misled the investigation. We don't know. We just know he could have."

"We don't know everything," Kay says, "but based on what we do know I think it's most likely that some combination of Eric and Justice and Jessica did it and helped cover it up. They were all downtown that night, lurking, up to no good. They're the only kids who were part of the trial who wouldn't take a polygraph test. All the other kids did. They all had means and opportunity, we just don't know what the motive was, but my guess is Angel stumbled on something they were doing, saw or heard something, or Eric just lost it."

I nod and think about it. "It's unusual for so many polygraphs to be given. Especially to witnesses. How'd that come about?"

Mary Elizabeth says, "When the investigation wasn't going anywhere and it became obvious they were going to scapegoat Qwon . . . we just thought . . . Kathryn said we can prove Qwon couldn't have done it. It was a strategy to get the police to stop wasting their time and energy on an innocent boy. His defense team set it up but it was independently conducted. But did the police listen to it, to actual evidence, for a single second? Of course not."

"Bottom line," Buck Diaz says, "we know Qwon wasn't involved. We know Justice Witney was. Just find out if he killed my little girl or helped someone else cover it up. We need to know for sure. We need to know who all was involved and exactly who did what. That's all we need to know, but we need to know for sure."

I can tell there's something sinister behind what he's saying.

"Why's that?" I ask.

"I'm an old man," he says. "Growin' older by the minute. I'll gladly trade my life for the lives of those who took my little girl from me and her mother, but I have to be sure. Once I know for sure . . . their time of walking around, enjoying this life like they didn't destroy the most precious thing in the world to us is over. Swear to Christ it's over in that hour."

Chapter Sixteen

On my drive home I listen to the episode of *Wrongful Conviction* about Angel's car.

"Welcome to another edition of *Wrongful Conviction*. I'm your host, Natasha Phillips. Today we're going to be talking about Angel's car. As you know Angel was never found, but her car was. But it wasn't found right away. It was found nearly a month after she went missing. Where was it all that time? Why wasn't if found sooner—or was it? Who parked it where it was? Now, supposedly Justice Witney took police to Angel's car. In fact, a lot of people find him to be credible primarily because of the fact that he knew where the car was—well, that and the cellphone evidence that backs up his statements. Some of his statements, I should say. Anyway, I say supposedly because our guest tonight has serious questions about whether Justice really led the cops to the car. And speaking of our guest . . . tonight we're joined by Nancy Drury of the *Nancy Drury Woman Detective Blog*. Welcome, Nancy."

I swerve to the side of the road, nearly hitting another car and almost running into the ditch.

Pausing the show, I call Merrick.

"I'm listening to the Wrongful Conviction podcast," I say.

"That's good stuff. I—"

"Nancy Drury is on it," I say.

"I know. She was on several. Really made a name for herself in true crime circles. I heard her on several before we got her letter and invited her onto ours. It came out quite a while before she was on our show, before . . . everything."

"I . . . I wasn't expecting to hear her. It was shocking."

"I can imagine," he says. "Sorry. You okay? Would've warned you if I had known."

"We should reach out to every show she was on," I say. "Interview them about her. See if they know anything that can help us."

"Already did," he says. "They all knew even less than us. Far as I can tell she never said anything that would give any kind of clue as to where she might be. I've also been monitoring true crime podcasts and blogs to see if I recognize her voice or writing style, even if it's under a different name."

"Wow," I say. "That's . . . really . . . great work, Merrick. Guess I'm just a little slow on the uptake."

"This just happens to be my area right now," he says. "I figure if we all work on what comes to us and in our areas, eventually one of us will come across something that leads us to her or to Daniel."

"Absolutely, but . . . this demonstrates why we should coordinate, get together occasionally, share what we have, brainstorm on other avenues of inquiry."

"Sounds good to me," he says. "Not used to cops sharing info."

"Sorry about that. But this is a special case. I know Merrill is working it hard too. We'll try to find out who else is and set up a meeting."

"Just let me know when and where. I'll be there."

We end the call and I turn back on the podcast and sit there on the shoulder of the highway listening for a few moments.

"Thanks for having me," Nancy says. "It's a pleasure to be here. I find this case fascinating and I love your show."

"It's great to have you on," Natasha says. "I read your blog religiously."

It's surreal to hear her voice again, to be sitting here listening to her talk about the very case I'm working on right now, and I find it disconcerting.

"So let's talk about Angel's car, shall we?" Natasha says.

"We shall," Nancy says.

"On January 16, 1999 when Angel Diaz went missing, so did her car," Natasha says. "This led some to conclude that she had runaway."

"Exactly," Nancy says. "In fact, her classmates stopped looking for her the night she went missing because her car was gone too and they thought she just decided to go home. According to several statements given by family and friends, she would do that—just leave when she got tired, often not saying anything to anyone, including goodbye."

Checking to see what's coming, I pull back onto the highway and continue listening to the person I'm searching for as I continue my journey back home.

"Right," Natasha says, "I've heard the same thing from several people. Her car was missing too, so it wasn't an unreasonable assumption that she just took off, but the police didn't handle it as if that's what happened. They treated this like an actual missing persons case—even earlier than they ordinarily would have, right? I mean, I thought they wouldn't consider someone Angel's age with a car missing until forty-eight hours or so, but the next morning when Angel's parents contacted the police, they came right out, took the report and started looking for her. Do you have any idea why?"

"I think I do," Nancy says. "Sex trafficking in or actually through Florida was getting a lot of attention at the time."

"I know. I worked on several stories about it."

"Yes you did. Won some awards for it, didn't you? Anyway . . . it wasn't just Eastern Block girls being brought in. American girls were being taken from right here in Florida. Some of the hotspots for sex trafficking at the time were Pensacola, Jacksonville, Tampa, and Miami. And there were stories not only about what was happening with sex slaves being moved to and through these places, but some young girls from around them being taken, too. About a month before Angel disappeared, a seventeen year-old girl vanished from Ft. Walton Beach and was later found chained to a bed in a Pensacola brothel. So I think that's one reason cops acted so fast."

"Wow," Natasha says. "You're probably right. That makes sense. They wanted to make sure she hadn't been taken by the sex traffickers."

"The other reason," Nancy says, "and the one that's far more likely, is that another Panama City girl, a sixteen year-old who attended Mosley, had been killed in October of the previous year—so less than three months from when Angel went missing—and her case was still unsolved at the time. Later, her boyfriend, a twenty-year-old student at Gulf Coast, confessed, but at the time it was unsolved and I think the police involved wanted to make sure the two cases weren't related, make sure they didn't have a serial killer on their hands."

"Wow," Natasha says again. "I had no idea. That makes perfect—explains why the cops responded the way they did. You're really good at this, Nancy. Thanks again for being on my show and sharing this with my listeners."

"Happy to be. Thanks for having me."

"We don't have time to discuss it today," Natasha says, "but you raise an interesting point and that is . . . could a serial killer have abducted and killed Angel Diaz? It's a statistical long shot, but something we should consider . . . given the sophistication of this crime. It being eighteen years and we still don't have a body. What do you think, Nancy?"

"I think we have to look at everything in every case. Anything less is sloppy and lazy and like too many official investigations where one suspect is focused on too early, to the exclusion of others."

"So let's have you back on to talk about psychopathic killers another time," Natasha says. "For today, let's stick with Angel's car. So the police are looking for Angel and her car from Sunday morning, the seventeenth. But they didn't find it until the fifteenth of February. Panama City is a relatively small town. Why wasn't Angel's car found sooner?"

"It could've been hidden, of course," Nancy says, "but I don't think it was. I, however, think it was moved around during that time. The thing is . . . we know at least one PCPD patrol officer and two Bay County Sheriff's deputies found the car and called it in."

"Think about that," Natasha says. "Three different law enforcement officers ran the plates on Angel's car during the month it was missing. How can that be? Wait for it. Wait for it. Nancy?"

"The PCPD officer who took the missing persons report from Angel's parents wrote down the tag number wrong or maybe they mistakenly gave it to him that way. Either way the tag was wrong on the form. So when it was called in, it didn't come back as belonging to Angel, which is more tragic than anything else, but what is interesting is that those three calls came from three different places around town, meaning . . . the car was being moved during that time."

"Any theories why?" Natasha asks.

"Haven't a clue," Nancy says. "But if we could figure out why, we might be able to figure out who— and the *who* is either the killer or someone helping him cover it up."

"Yes," Natasha says. "Let's do that. Now . . . eventually the mistake was realized, the form fixed, and Angel's car was found in long term parking at the Panama City airport one day short of a month since she first went missing."

"And we're talking about the old airport," Nancy says. "The one in town, not the new one out in the middle of nowhere."

"Right. So let's talk about what was in it."

"And what was not," Nancy adds.

"Exactly. So Acqwon Lewis's prints were all in the vehicle."

"As you'd expect them to be," Nancy says. "The two had dated for six months or so and he'd been in the car several times. But guess what wasn't in the car."

"Any of Justice Witney's prints," Natasha says. "Which contradicts his statements to the police."

"He claims he wiped his side down but there are prints all over that side, so if he'd have wiped it down they wouldn't be there."

"We're not sure what else Justice Witney is, but we know he's a liar," Natasha says.

"The driver's side had been wiped down some—the steering wheel, gearshift, door handles, turn signal," Nancy says. "What you'd expect to see if the killer or someone attempting to help him cover up the crime had driven the car."

"Exactly. Which, if it were Qwon, wouldn't you think he'd wipe down the entire car? He had to know his prints were all in it."

"Unless, in the heat of the moment, he wasn't thinking that clearly and didn't realize how many he was leaving," Nancy says, "but the fact that the car was moved so much argues against that because whoever moved it had to wipe it down each time. Surely if it was Qwon he would've thought about his prints being all in the car at some point and wiped the entire car down. Or burned it or driven it into the bay."

"There were signs of violence in the car," Natasha says. "Like a struggle had taken place there. So it was assumed that's where Angel was killed. Several of the knobs for the AC, radio, et cetera had been kicked off and were laying in the floorboard. The turn signal or wiper handle—there's conflicting reports—had been broken and was dangling down. Some of Angel's blood was found in the car, which you might expect—it really wasn't a lot—and in the trunk, which you probably wouldn't expect. There wasn't a ton of blood in either place, but there was more in the trunk."

"The theory is she was killed in her car and then her body was placed in the trunk and remained there for a while so there's more blood in it."

"Angel's car had the normal teenage stuff you'd expect to find," Natasha says. "CDs, school text books, random clothes and shoes, gum and candy wrappers, fast food cups and bags and trash, a few soda bottles, but nothing very revealing or incriminating. Qwon had a couple of shirts in the backseat."

"Which, again, if he did it, you'd think he would've taken," Nancy says.

"True. Now let's talk about one of the more interesting things found in Angel's car. There was a mileage log. Angel worked for Dominos and delivered pizza, which she was paid mileage for. She also worked part-time as a courier for a law office downtown, which she was also paid milage for. She got into the habit of recording all her miles in her log and she was meticulous about it."

"Which means," Nancy says, "we know how many miles were put on her car after she and it went missing."

"And it's not a small number," Natasha adds.

"No it's not. Nearly six hundred miles, which means the car was used and moved a lot in the month after Angel went missing."

"Somebody was using it to the tune of about twenty miles a day," Natasha says. "Which seems like a very big risk."

"Unless," Nancy says, "he knew the police had the wrong tag number."

"How could he know something like that?" Natasha asks.

"One obvious way," Nancy says, "would be if his dad was a cop."

Chapter Seventeen

"Yeah, my father was a cop back then," Eric Pulsifer says. "But two things. One, I didn't do anything, so there was nothing for him to cover up and two, he was a patrol cop. He couldn't have done anything on one of the detectives' investigations anyway—even if he wanted to, which he didn't, 'cause I didn't do anything."

Doesn't mean he didn't have a buddy who was a detective who did it for him, but I don't mention it.

It's the afternoon of the next day. I spent the morning in meetings with Reggie at the sheriff's department about, among other things, finding Daniel.

Unlike the awkward, unfortunate looking teenage boy he had been, Eric Puller is now an average mid-thirties man who wears expensive casual clothes and plenty of aftershave. His hair isn't as red now and much more closely cropped, his freckles have faded some, and stubble helps define his puffy face and conceal his nearly nonexistent chin. He's the manager of a seafood restaurant in Mexico Beach, the small coastal town between Port St. Joe and Panama City on Highway 98.

The restaurant, the Shrieking Gull, sits on the Gulf side, a huge wooden structure with a large deck and a crow's nest bar up a narrow staircase. We're sit-

ting on a wooden bench behind the kitchen, facing the
Gulf as we talk.

It's offseason. The little lunch crowd is long
gone, the restaurant mostly or maybe completely
empty. The sun is high in the sky, the February day is
bright but cool, the breeze blowing in off the water
biting. Beneath the clear, cloudless sky, the green Gulf
is calm, its sea foam whitecaps lining the surf like the
wrinkled forehead of a furrowed brow.

"When'd you change your name?" I ask.

Something flashes in his eyes then is gone, and
I'm not sure what it is—anger? pain? embarrassment?
Perhaps a complex mixture of all three.

"Long time ago now," he says, squinting his
eyes, seeming to think about it. "Wow. I've been
Puller nearly as long as I was the other." He shakes his
head slowly. "Can't believe how quickly my life is flying by."

It's not lost on me that he can't even say *Pulsifer*, and I wonder exactly why that is. But I don't have
to wonder for long.

"High school was hell for me," he says. "Far
worse when Angel dumped me. Most of the kids
thought I was weird and I guess I was a little. But . . .
really it was just a little . . . I was just a little different.
Awkward. Uncomfortable. Shy. But goddamn the
price they make you pay for that. The cruelty was . . .
severe. I knew what they thought of me. I tried to be
different, tried to fit in, but everything I did backfired,
made it all worse. They called me Pussifer and Eric

Pussyface and all kind of other names right in front of me. It was . . ."

"I'm very sorry," I say.

He looks at me, the painful memories burning in his eyes. "Are you?"

I nod. "I really am."

"Would you be just as much if I killed Angel?"

I don't respond. Doesn't feel like I need to— question seemed either rhetorical or intended to get a reaction.

"Sorry," he says. "It's just . . . reliving all this shit is . . . tough."

It's obvious he still has a lot of unresolved pain and anger associated with the hell that was high school for him.

"You know I can count on one hand the kids who were decent to me in high school. Qwon was one of them. So was his sister—*and* her boyfriend. And Angel—even after we broke up. That's it."

"You ever talked to anyone about it?" I ask. "Or written about it? Tried processing it in any way?"

He doesn't respond, just looks out at the Gulf and says, "I've made a good life for myself. Doin' good. Got a wife who doesn't think I'm a pussy. Got a daughter who adores me. Got a decent job and want for nothing essential. I'm happy."

He may be happy, but just beneath it is a toxic concoction of pain and anger and regret and frustration, rot behind the walls of the partial remodeling he's done.

"I'm glad," I say. "That's all great. But it'd be even better if you experienced some healing relating to the other."

He shakes his head and waves off what I'm saying. "I'm good. The past is the past. It's in the past."

"Actually, it's not."

He lets out a harsh, mean little laugh. "Guess you're right. Goddamn podcasts and blogs and TV shows all think I did it. Some of 'em come right out and say so. It's like bein' back then all over again. Except . . . my wife and daughter don't know about it. Nor does anyone here at work. Nobody in my life knows Eric Puller used to be Eric Pulsifer and I intend to keep it that way."

I nod.

"People say I was stalkin' her, that I followed her around downtown that night, that she came over to confront me and I killed her. I did . . . I didn't stalk anyone. Not like that. I was just lost. Didn't know what to do with myself. So I always looked for Angel, knowing she'd be nice to me. But . . ."

"What do you remember about that night?" I ask.

His eyes narrow and he looks up as if trying to access memories he's long since buried deep. "Being alone. Being lonely. Just wanting to join in and have a good time like everyone else was, but . . . I . . . when I saw Angel wasn't at Fiesta I didn't stay long. I heard she and some others had already gone over to Kim and Ken's, so I decided to. When I walked out, Qwon came out too. At first I thought he was heading to

Kim and Ken's too, but when I looked back he was walking around toward the front of the building. Then Kathryn came out and yelled after him, 'Grab my jacket too' or something like that. I kept walkin'. When I neared Kim and Ken's, I saw that Angel was leaving, like . . . heading straight toward me, going back toward downtown or Fiesta or whatever. I said hi but I kept walkin' toward Kim and Ken's. Didn't want her thinking I was following her or anything. She walked back up Beach Drive the way I had just come. Instead of going into Kim and Ken's I kept walkin' up their street, made the block, and walked back into downtown the long way around—over to Cherry, then Cove and around. Took forever. By the time I got downtown I just decided to go home. So I did."

"Anybody see you?"

"What part of lonely and alone do you not understand?"

"What about once you got home?"

"Dad was on patrol. Mom was already in bed."

"What do you think happened to Angel?"

"I know what happened," he says. "It's obvious. Qwon was outside. Went to get something out of the car or whatever. Probably drugs. Angel was walking back in that direction the last time I saw her. He said something or did something and she saw it. They got into a fight and he killed her. I have no idea how or why or any of the details, but that's what happened and that's why Justice Witney's testimony is true and backed up by the cellphone records. That's why you're wasting your time. And so is everybody else on those

stupid shows and shit. And remember what I said.
Qwon was nice to me. I liked him. I don't want it to
be him, but it was. Good people sometimes do very
bad things."

Chapter Eighteen

"If he did it and let Qwon take the blame for it all these years, that's some cold shit," Darius Turner says. "Qwon, Katie, and me were about the only ones that were nice to him."

"He said y'all were."

Darius Turner, Qwon's best friend and Kathryn's boyfriend back in high school, works for Ace Hardware and is in town to help set up the new store. He's staying at the Dead Lakes Campground where Anna and I brought the girls on Saturday. We're sitting in two lawn chairs in front of his camper. He's drinking a Bud Light. I'm sipping on an ice-cold bottle of water.

He's a trim, muscular, mid-thirties black man with a roundish face, closely cropped, receding hair, and large eyes. He's wearing black slacks and a red Polo shirt with the Ace Hardware logo on it.

"And Angel, of course," he adds. He then shakes his head and frowns. "She was a good person. Had all these . . . I don't know . . . like strong convictions about what's right and shit. Always did the right thing as far as I ever saw. Can't believe this happened to her."

"Eric said she was nice to him even after she broke up with him."

He nods. "She was. Really was. She was good people. We all were. Had a good little group. Think maybe part of it was the racial thing. Our group was somewhat diverse and we knew what it was like to suffer ignorance at the hands of bullies and haters."

I nod.

"Tell me about your group," I say.

"Well, it was bigger than just the four of us, but that's who I was talking about right then. It's funny, you're so young back then you can't really appreciate shit. You . . . I guess you have nothing to compare it to, but the older I get, the more people I get to know, the more relationships I have . . . I don't know . . . I guess I just realize how good we had it. I've never had another friend like Qwon, never had another girlfriend as good as Katie. Sorry, *Kathryn*. Kathryn and I never had a cross word. Not once. We just . . . it was just so good. I think the only reason we broke up was because of what happened to Angel and Qwon. And they had a good relationship too. More turbulent than ours, but still good. Real good compared to most relationships I see these days. We were all close. Qwon and Kathryn were good friends. Made it possible for us all to be. I'm sure we had the normal teenage insecurities and angst, but we didn't have all the anger and resentment and ulterior motives and pettiness you find in adults. Just wasn't there. Guess maybe that's all sort of beside the point, isn't it?"

He pauses. I nod, encouraging him to continue, which he does.

"Going back to Eric," he says. "I don't think he had violence in him toward anyone, but especially us. Especially Angel. He never so much as gave a dirty look to those cruel bastards who were making fun of and bullying him back then. Don't see him hurting anyone. Angel least of all. Don't see him letting Qwon take the fall for him if he did it. I know guys like him sometimes just snap and go off on somebody—sometimes somebody close to them, but . . . I just don't see it."

"Who do you think did it?" I ask.

"I know Qwon didn't. Know he couldn't have. We were with him all night. If Justice didn't do it, there's only two other people I think it could be, but I think Justice killed her or helped someone do it or helped someone cover it up. At a minimum he's involved."

"Who're the other two?"

"Well, they're exes," he says. "Eric, but like I said I don't think he had it in him. Or Zelda."

"Zelda?"

"Qwon's ex. She was one crazy bitch. No one's ever really mentioned her. Don't know if the police even investigated her, but she was nuts. They weren't even together that long—didn't take him long to find out how crazy she was, but she acted like they were Romeo and Juliet or some shit."

"What's her last name? Was she in your class?"

He thinks about it. "Sager. That's it. Zelda Sager. Think she was in our class or the one behind us at one point but she dropped out. I remember she smelled funny . . . . like she ate funky food or some shit like that. She was out there. Sort of like a hippie or a . . . that's what—she acted like a Manson girl. Something like that. Told Qwon she'd die for him. I remember that."

"Any idea where she is now?"

He shakes his head. "Haven't seen her since back then. And . . . look . . . I'm not accusing her or Eric. I don't even know if she was downtown that night. Don't remember seeing her. She just came to mind because she's so—was so . . . weird. My money's still on Justice."

Chapter Nineteen

When I get home a prosecutor for the State's Attorney's office is waiting for me.

He's actually outside on one of the metal yard chairs beneath the pergola, as if Anna wouldn't let him in the house.

When I approach him, he stands and introduces himself as Denny Conroy. He's a trim young man with pale skin and ice blue eyes beneath thick black hair.

"I'm on my way to Panama City," he says, "and I wanted to stop by and tell you and your—whatever Ms. Rodden is to you—in person that Chris Taunton is being released. Probably be out in a week or so. Maybe sooner."

"Do you want to come in?" I ask.

He shakes his head. "Spend my life inside—offices, courtrooms, cars. Sit outside any chance I get. Y'all've got a nice place here. Pretty yard and lake. Nice little town. I've just been sitting here enjoying it."

The side door opens and Anna comes out with Taylor on her hip.

I hug and kiss them both.

I look back at Denny. "What she is to me," I say, "is everything."

The expression he gives me is the restrained, polite equivalent of rolling his eyes, but I don't care.

It's casting pearls before swine, and to say anything else would be like trying to explain poetry, so I let it go.

Anna says, "Did you talk to your boss about moving forward with the case and blaming John if it fails?"

He nods. "He wouldn't go for it. Oh, he's still gonna blame your—he's gonna blame John, but . . . we're cutting our losses now. No sense in throwing good money after bad. Sometimes . . . them's the breaks."

"Careful not to be too flippant," she says. "You're talking about the man who not only cheated on me repeatedly during our marriage but then tried to have us killed."

"Sorry. I didn't mean any . . . I'm sorry it worked out this way. I truly am. I's lookin' forward to gettin' the sorry, slick bastard in court." He looks at Taylor and adds, "Excuse my French."

Anna shakes her head and frowns, but it's not over his French. "It's a weak, dick move to not bring the case and to blame John."

"I realize it's not what y'all want to hear, and I'm not saying I agree with it, but . . . I'm not the boss. It's not my call."

Merrill pulls into the driveway then eases onto the grass on the right side so as not to block in the car with the Leon County tag on it. I had done the same thing—our driveway is long and straight and runs up the side of the house and isn't wide enough to turn around on.

As he walks toward us I can see he's carrying a large file folder containing the case notes he received from the Freedom of Information Act request he made in the Angel Diaz investigation.

"I know it's something else y'all don't want to hear," Denny says, "but building a case isn't easy, but it's essential to getting a conviction. Next time . . . let professionals who aren't involved with the suspect's wife handle the investigation."

Merrill shakes his head and lets out a harsh laugh as he walks up.

Denny turns toward him. "You got something to say?"

"Nothing you want to hear," Merrill says, smiling as he uses Denny's own phrase against him. "Just sick as shit of weak ass bastards blaming the victims. John didn't *handle* the case. Didn't ask to be hunted or have his wife abducted. These good people woke up inside a sociopath's nightmare and not only survived but took him down. They did all you could ask them to do. Don't stand there in our town on their property making excuses for your ballsack of a boss for not doing his small part. Now, if you'll excuse us . . . the adults have some work to do."

Without waiting for a response, Merrill walks inside the house.

Anna turns and follows.

"You gave me some unsolicited advice," I say, "so I'm gonna return the favor. It'd be a good investment of your time to ask yourself if you were the boss . . . if you'd've made a different call. I appreciate you coming by to tell us in person. Shows character your boss doesn't have. So maybe the answer is yes. I sincerely hope so. Have a good day."

I extend my hand and he shakes it, and we leave it at that.

Chapter Twenty

"Brought you something," Merrill says when I walk in.

He holds up the file folder.

Our home is a late 60s ranch, and the side entrance we use leads through a small mudroom into a galley kitchen. Merrill is standing at the end of the kitchen in the eating area close to the high cypress table.

"Just what I wanted. Thank you. Have you looked at it?"

"Time or two," he says.

"You feel like giving me your thoughts while I unload the dishwasher?"

While Anna puts Taylor to bed, I unload the dishwasher, and Merrill sits at the table, a Corona Light in hand, the file open before him, and gives me his thoughts on it.

"Be interesting to see how what's in here compares to what's in the defense file Kathryn gave you," he says.

"Yes it will."

"My guess is prosecution didn't turn over everything to the defense. But now that the case is closed I bet we got more from the FOIA request."

I try to place the dishes into the cabinets as gently and quietly as possible so I don't disturb Taylor or Sam, but the plates are heavy and have a tendency to be loud.

"Oh shit," Merrill says. "Almost forgot. Found Jessica Poole."

"You did?"

I had asked him to see if he could find Justice's coconspirator, who had so far eluded us.

"Changed her name to Jennifer Polk and moved to Michigan," he says.

"Nothing suspicious about that," I say.

"Died of a drug overdose about ten years back," he says.

"Shit," I say.

"Ain't it?"

My response is nearly equal parts sadness for Jessica's short, sad life and frustration at not being able to interview her.

We might still be able to determine exactly what, if any, her involvement was, but we won't be able to do it through her.

"You know how the cops first go on Qwon and narrowed in on him so fast?"

"How's that?"

"Anonymous tip," he says. "Call came in early on in the investigation. Hell, she'd only been missing a few days, still weeks before her car was found, but someone called and said Qwon did it. They were looking at him anyway, boyfriend and all, but once they got that call . . . don't think they looked at anyone else."

I nod and think about it as I dry some excess water left in the cups and place them in the cabinet.

"You domesticated as fuck now, aren't you?" he says.

I smile the smile of a truly happily married man.

Which is exactly what I am, even though we haven't made it official yet. I've proposed and she accepted, but with my dad being sick and dealing with the girls and life and cases and Daniel going missing and Sam moving in with us, that's all that's happened so far. I've been looking at rings and we've discussed some possible dates, but haven't settled on either yet.

He shakes his head. "You hatin' this briar patch you been thrown in, ain't you?"

"With a passion."

"Been thinkin' 'bout seein' if Za and I can find one to jump into together," he says.

"One what?" Anna asks, walking in and placing the baby monitor on the counter beside the stove.

"Whatever this is you and John have mired yourselves in."

"Don't wait. Do it as soon as you can."

She begins to pull out a few pots and pans, attempting to do it as quietly as possible.

"That's what I was about to say."

"Maybe I keep bringin' her 'round y'all, the idea'll occur to her," he says.

"Bet it already has," Anna says. "What time will she be here?"

"Half an hour or so," he says. "Time enough for us to solve this case."

"I have some thoughts to share on that too," Anna says. "What did I miss while I was putting Taylor down?"

He tells her.

"Any idea who this anonymous tipster was?" she asks.

"I just might," he says. "Did I mention there was a Crime Stoppers reward? Angel's family and friends raised money and donated it to Crime Stoppers and . . . wait for it . . . there was a payout."

"Do we know how much, when, and to whom?" Anna says.

"The who is all anonymous and shit," he says, "but the when and how much ain't. And guess what? The when and the how much may just tell us the who. The way it's supposed to work is the anonymous tipster receives a cash reward when there is an arrest or grand jury indictment of a felony offender."

"So when Qwon was arrested . . ." Anna says.

"Supposed to have been then, but it wasn't. Angel went missing on January 16, 1999. The anonymous tip came in on the following Tuesday, the day after MLK day, January 19th. Angel's car was found on February 15th. Qwon was arrested on February 20th, but the Crime Stoppers payout didn't take place until . . . June of . . . 2000."

"A year and a half later?" Anna says.

"Almost."

"Why?"

"The only explanation I can come up with," Merrill says, "is . . . that's around the time Justice Witney was released from prison for the little hand slap he received for helping Qwon destroy Angel's body, aiding and abetting a felon, and obstructing justice."

"*He* was the anonymous tipster?" Anna says, her voice rising several steps.

"I think so."

"It fits," I say. "Makes a certain sense."

"That's the problem with giving cash rewards for anonymous tips," Anna says. "I see the need for it, but it almost causes more trouble than it's worth. It's supposed to protect witnesses from retaliation, which is needed—especially in areas with gangs and organized crime—but it's abused all the time. Used by cops to pay their informants. Used by other criminals to direct suspicion at an enemy or just make a little blood money. There have been multiple cases where not only was the tipster lying but the cops actually got him to falsely confess to being part of the crime. Innocent people, including the tipsters themselves, have done decades in prison only to be later exonerated by DNA."

"It can be extremely helpful in an investigation," I say, "but it's a system rife with abuse."

"If it's true Justice was the tipster," Anna says, "then Qwon will almost certainly get a new trial."

"Why's that?" Merrill says.

"The defense and court and jury never knew about it," she says. "You can't have a witness benefiting financially like that and not disclose it to the court.

They got around it by not having him claim the reward until a year and a half later. It's possible the cops didn't even tell the prosecution who the tipster was so he could get away with not disclosing it, keep him from committing a Brady violation."

"What's a Brady violation?" Merrill asks.

"The Brady doctrine deals with pretrial discovery," she says. "Comes from Brady v. Maryland back in . . . 1963 I believe. Supreme Court ruled that the prosecution is required to turn over all exculpatory evidence, anything impeachable, to the defendant in a criminal case before the trial starts."

"Exculpatory?" Merrill says.

"Evidence that might exonerate the defendant," she says. "Such as your star witness is getting a reward for his testimony, or DNA or fingerprints not belonging to the defendant was found at the crime scene, or a witness came forward and claimed the defendant was with him. Evidence that might exonerate a defendant or be used to impeach other witnesses or evidence. It all has to be turned over pretrial. If it's not, it's grounds for a new trial."

"But finding proof it was him . . ." Merrill says.

"Yeah," she says. "Will be next to impossible."

"Maybe we don't have to," I say. "Maybe we just prove he did it and lied about Qwon being involved . . . which more and more is what it's looking like."

Chapter Twenty-one

When Zaire Bell, Merrill's M.D. main squeeze, arrives, Merrill and I are on the back patio grilling steaks and Anna is making a salad in the kitchen.

She's a tall, fit but thick in all the right places, forty-something African-American woman with smooth skin the color of caramelized sugar, intelligent, dark eyes that shimmer as if she's seeing things no one else is, large, luscious brown lips, and wavy, natural hair that extends some six inches from her head.

After talking to Anna for a moment, she steps out onto the patio.

She is brilliant and beautiful and seems perfect for Merrill. I'm grateful for Sacred Heart Hospital bringing her up here from Miami and couldn't be happier for them.

"Smells so good," she says. "Times like these I wish I wasn't a vegetarian."

I spin around to look at her, my eyes wide, but she has a huge smile on her face.

She and Merrill start laughing.

"She's just fuckin' with you," he says. "This girl loves meat—and lots of it."

I can tell he's talking about her actual eating habits—I've never heard him make a comment like that about anyone he's dating—but she thinks he means it as a double entendre and turns and punches him.

"Damn," he says. "All that red meat in her diet makes her hostile and aggressive."

"I'm gonna take this hostility and aggression into the kitchen and channel it toward helping Anna."

She and Merrill kiss again and she is gone.

I lift the lid on the grill and flip the steaks.

"You worried about the bullshit the State's attorney's gonna do?" he asks.

I shake my head. "Don't look forward to it, but . . . it's nothing compared to us having to deal with Chris."

"Can't believe that bastard's gettin' out."

I don't respond. There's nothing to say.

Eventually I say, "Did you come across the name Zelda Sager in any of the Angel Diaz case notes?"

He shakes his head. "Who's she?"

"Qwon's ex-girlfriend. Darius said she was crazy and crazy obsessed. Just wondered if the police ever even talked to her."

I pull the steaks off the grill and we head inside.

"Cops didn't talk to much of anybody," he says as he closes the door behind us. Not PCPD or Bay County Sheriff. Early on—I mean very early on they liked Qwon for it and . . ."

"What's not to like?" Za says. "Black guy. Dating a white girl. Only thing surprising is he's not on death row."

A small wood fire in the fire place crackles and hisses, and the room is warm. Sam opens her eyes drowsily. Merrill smiles at her and touches her hand.

Everything else is waiting on the table. I place the steaks down in the center and the four of us sit down to eat.

Sam is back asleep. She had another surgery recently and is sleeping a lot more these days. A small stereo on the table next to her bed plays soothing music with nature sounds that helps calm and comfort her. The volume is very low and barely audible in the dining area.

Next to the stereo on the bedside table is a picture of Daniel. We hesitated to put it there. We're still not sure if he was abducted or chose to leave and stay gone on his own. But Sam's not aware of any of that—or even that he's missing—so we decided the comfort she'd receive from having it there outweighed any damage or eventual undoing of anything if Daniel is found dead or decides never to return.

"This is so good," Za says. "Thanks for having us over—*and* for cooking this great food." She glances at Sam. "I don't see how you do it all. We should be havin' y'all over."

"I'll tell you how she does it all," I say. "And with such grace. She's a truly extraordinary woman."

"She is that," Za says.

"That's very sweet," Anna says, "but let's change the subject." She looks at Merrill. "After reading the case file, do you still think Qwon's guilty?"

He shrugs. "More I see . . . more I think he might be . . . innocent. It was a sloppy, narrowly focused investigation, a weak defense at trial, and . . . this guy Justice . . . By my count he's told six different stories, changes his statement six different times."

Anna and I nod.

Za says, "But doesn't that usually mean someone is telling the truth? I thought if a statement was exactly the same every time it was because it was memorized and not true."

"You might expect some things to be mentioned one time and not another—like memory issues," Merrill says, "or maybe for him to be willing to reveal more as he went along, but his story actually changes. The statements actually contradict each other. And not only on little shit either."

"I've read them too," Anna says. "And I agree. He's lying. Some experts think the first statement is generally the most true, but he says next to nothing the first time."

"And the investigators are leading him every time," I say.

Merrill says, "You notice the times he was logged at the station versus when they started recording the interviews?"

I nod.

"What?" Za asks.

"Each time he was there a couple of hours or more before they started recording the interview," Merrill says.

"Coaching him on what to say," Anna adds.

"Oh."

"In the interviews you can tell when he forgets to say something they told him to be sure to include," Merrill says. "They'll remind him, say some shit like 'I thought you said previously . . .' then he apologizes and adds it in."

"It's like it took them six times to get the statement they wanted," Anna says. "Kept massaging it, editing, rehearsing, coaching, leading."

Merrill nods. "That's the single biggest reason I think Qwon might be innocent. That and the witness statements that say he was downtown with them the whole time."

"Yeah," Anna says, "you'd expect his sister and best friend to lie for him, but not the entire group and not for eighteen years."

"And didn't you say they all passed poly-graphs?" Za says.

Merrill nods. "Just like Qwon."

"All that together is pretty compelling and con-vincing," Anna says.

"We need to talk to Justice," I say.

"I've been lookin' for him," Merrill says. "Motherfucker vanished off the face of the planet."

"I'll tell you another thing that needs a closer look and that's the cellphone evidence," Anna says. "There are serious questions about it in general. I think a lot of courts have concluded it's just not reli-able for determining exactly where someone is. I'll keep working on that."

"What can I do?" Za asks. "I want to be a member of the Scooby gang."

We all laugh.

"I'm serious."

"You could read the case file Merrill has," I say. "See what stands out to you that we've missed. And you could try to locate Qwon's crazy ex-girlfriend Zelda Sager."

Chapter Twenty-two

The next morning I search for Qwon in confinement, but he's not there. When I can't find him in his dorm or work assignment, I grow concerned.

Eventually I find him in the infirmary.

His face is bruised and swollen, his eyes bloodshot, and his head is wrapped in a large white bandage.

"What happened?" I ask.

He shrugs slowly and moans a little as he does. "Got jumped. Couple of guys with a lock in a sock."

Nearly all weapons in prison are improvised weapons—and among them, a combination lock inside a long sock is among the most popular. Easier to make, use, and hide than a shiv, a lock in a sock delivers fast and furious blunt force trauma using two items nearly every inmate has.

"Any idea who?" I ask.

He frowns and shakes his head. "I've never had anything like this happen before. Everybody—COs and the other inmates—seem to like me. I never do anything to anyone. Never get mixed up in any bullshit. Keep my nose clean. I'm friendly to everyone."

"No idea why it happened, what the motive could be?"

"No, sir. I'll be honest with you, even if I knew who did it, I wouldn't tell you. All that'd do is get me killed, but if I had any idea why, I'd tell you. I just genuinely have no idea."

"Where'd it happen?" I ask. "How?"

"I'd just been released from confinement," he says. "This was last night about seven, I guess. I was on my way back to my dorm, had all my property in a big garbage bag. I had only taken a few steps out of the confinement building when they jumped me. Just . . . one of them tackled me and the other started beating me with the lock in the sock. When the one who had tackled me was on his feet again he started kicking me. I tried to get up, but I couldn't. Eventually, I just got in a sort of fetal position and tried to protect my head and midsection."

"Did they say anything?"

He shakes his head and winces. "No, sir. No message or anything. Just put a whoopin' on me and took off."

"Which officer was on duty when you were released?" I ask.

He glances at the glassed wall of the officers' station at the other end of the infirmary.

"Not sure," he says. "Can't remember. Don't think I had seen them before."

"Really?" I ask in surprise.

"Yes, sir."

"So if I check the log I won't see that it was Troy Payne?"

His eyes widen an almost imperceptible amount.

I nod. "Any idea why he has such a yen for you?"

"No, sir. Wish I did. I'd do my best to make it right. Far as I know . . . he's the only one here who has anything against me. I've tried to talk to him, but . . . he . . . I can't get anywhere."

"Do you want me to have you placed in protective management?" I say.

"No, sir. If . . . an—someone other than an inmate—is behind it they can get to me anywhere."

I nod. "I'll see what I can do about keeping you safe and gettin' to the bottom of this before anything else happens."

"Thank you. And thanks for coming to see me. How'd you hear I was in here so fast?"

"I didn't," I say. "I went to confinement, your dorm, and your work assignment looking for you first."

"How come? Has something happened?"

"Just had a few more questions for you," I say.

"About Angel?"

"About the case," I say, nodding.

"I'll tell you anything I can."

"Do you think Zelda could've done it?" I ask. "And set you up?"

"*Zelda*? Wow. That's a . . . Haven't heard that name in a lifetime or so. I'll be honest with you . . . I can't imagine anyone I know doing it—including Zelda. Nobody I know would want to hurt Angel—let alone kill her."

"Yet, somebody did," I say.

"Maybe not. Maybe she did just take off. That's what I like to think. She's happy somewhere."

"Even with you in here?"

He looks at me like it's obvious. "Of course. This is nothing compared to being brutally murdered."

"What makes you think it was brutal?"

He freezes for a moment, then shrugs. "Just an expression. The . . . just the thought of it is brutal to me, so . . ."

"You don't think Zelda could be violent?"

"I know firsthand she can be violent and vindictive," he says. "Turns out she was not a nice person, but . . . murder, actually ending someone's life . . . I don't see it."

"Any idea where she is now?" I ask.

"Absolutely none. Pretty much lost track of everybody when I was thrown into the belly of the beast."

"Same go for Justice Witney?" I say. "He's vanished too."

He nods. "Yes, sir. Haven't seen him since he testified against me at my trial."

"And you still haven't come up with any reasons why he did that?"

"No, sir. Sorry."

"Could he have done it for the money?" I ask.

"Money? What money?"

"Reward money."

"He got all the reward money Angel's family and friends raised?" he says, his voice rising. "Please tell me he didn't." He lets out a harsh little laugh.

"Wanna hear something tragic and ironic? I donated to it. Please tell me I didn't contribute to my own demise."

Chapter Twenty-three

That night Merrill and I ride to Apalach to follow up on a new lead relating to Randa and Daniel's disappearance.

As with every lead we've looked into so far nothing came of it. Someone thought they saw something—a woman who might be Randa, a man who might be Daniel, but it was neither, another dead end. Not a waste of time exactly—both because no time with Merrill is ever wasted and every dead end street we go down gets us closer to finding the street that Daniel is actually on.

The trip down to Apalach and our time there was uneventful, but what happens on the way back is the most eventful thing to happen in the case so far.

My phone rings and the readout on the screen says the number is blocked.

I answer.

"Hey John," Randa Raffield says.

I hesitate a second before saying, "Hey."

My mind races. What can I do? How can I trace the call? Track her down?

I reach over and punch Merrill on the arm repeatedly. When he looks at me I mouth to him who it is.

His eyes widen and he pulls out his phone and starts punching in numbers.

"How are you?" she asks.

"I'm good," I say. "But I miss my friend Daniel a lot."

"Not me?" she says. "Just Daniel?"

"No, I'd like to see you again too," I say.

"I hope you're not wasting even a second of your time trying to figure out a way to trace this call," she says. "If you don't give me more credit than that by now I'm not sure I can continue our association."

"All I'm doing is talking to you," I say.

"Good. 'Cause I'm on a burner phone, prepaid piece of shit I'll destroy after this call and I've routed it through several countries into yours, none of which are the one I'm in, so . . ."

Merrill pulls off the road onto the shoulder and quietly gets out of the car.

"Can't help but notice you said the country *you're* in, not *we're* in," I say. "Is Daniel no longer with you?"

"Thought we had a deal, John," she says. "You weren't going to look for me and I was going to take good care of Daniel."

"Are you?" I ask.

"What? Taking good care of Daniel? Are you looking for me?"

"Are you calling because you think I am?" I ask.

"No," she says. "I'm callin' because I know you are."

"Don't punish Daniel for what you think I'm doing," I say.

Merrill is standing in front of the car talking on the phone, his large frame in the headlights casting a long shadow on the damp shoulder of the road. I'm fairly certain he's talking to Reggie or someone about trying to trace the call to my phone. I'm completely certain it will do no good.

"What're you working on these days?" she asks. "I mean besides finding me and Daniel?"

"A few different things," I say. "Why?"

"Don't do that," she says. "Don't be vague. You know I'm asking about the Angel Diaz case."

How does she know? Does she have us bugged? Did she hack into our computers? I decide the latter is more likely. Our searches alone would let her know what we're up to.

"I listened to a podcast you were on about it," I say.

"You think you're smarter than me, don't you John?"

"Actually," I say, "I don't. It's not a competition, but . . . if it were, when we went head to head last time you won."

"I did, didn't I?"

"Wasn't even close."

"Think you would've figured it out eventually?" she says.

"Isn't that why you took off *and* took Daniel?"

"Was I right to?" she asks. "Were you getting close?"

"Yeah, but . . . you still had a little time. I wasn't about to knock on your door or anything."

She laughs.

"What if we do the reverse of the previous deal?" I say. "What if you let Daniel go and I don't try to find you?"

"You didn't keep the previous deal," she says.

"It wasn't a deal we agreed to. It was a request you left me in a note."

"A request?"

"Well, a demand."

"So if I let Daniel go, you'll leave me alone, not try to find me? But what if he doesn't want to go? What if I couldn't get rid of him if I wanted to? What if I like the idea of being pursued by you? But let's get back to what we were talking about earlier. I didn't solve the Angel Diaz case."

"Yeah?"

"So if you do does that mean you're smarter than me?"

"No."

"What if I'm still actively investigating it?" she says. "If we're both working it at the same time, would whoever solves it first be smarter?"

"Let's ask Daniel," I say. "Put him on the phone."

"Tell you what," she says. "New deal. One you'll actually keep if you agree to it."

"What's that?"

"We'll both work on the case," she says. "If you solve it first, I'll let Daniel go—whether he leaves or not is all him. If I solve the case first, you'll stop look-ing for us, leave us alone."

"The only way it'll be fair is if you have the case file," I say. "I'll mail you a copy. What's your address? Better yet, I'll bring it to you."

"Cute. Do we have a deal?"

"Let Daniel go and we'll stop looking for you," I say. "It's the best deal you're going to get."

"So you're scared of losing to me again?" she says.

"I just won't be able to stop looking for Daniel—even if you do win."

"It's so sweet that you won't lie to me," she says. "Wow. I . . . mean . . . just precious. It's precious. It really is. Tell you what . . . I'm a woman of my word too. So here's the best deal you're going to get. A to-tally insane, one-sided deal that only benefits you. If I solve the case before you, nothing happens—except it'll be Randa two, John zero, but if you solve it first I'll let Daniel go. And if you still just can't live without me you can keep trying to find me. Deal?"

"Deal."

"I'll even give you a hint," she says. "Qwon didn't do it."

Chapter Twenty-four

"I can't believe she called you," Anna says.

"Shows how confident she is," I say, "how safe she feels."

We are in my favorite place in the world—our bed—on our sides facing each other, talking softly in the dusky half-darkness.

"What'd she say exactly?"

I tell her—well, as exactly as I can recall.

"So she said very little about Daniel and wouldn't let you speak to him," she says. "Do you think he's even alive?"

"I do," I say, "but . . . it's not really based on anything."

"Why would she call?" she says. "What's her motivation? What does it benefit her?"

"I'm not sure exactly. Think it's part of her psychological makeup. She likes to talk. Think about how many podcasts she was on. *May still be on.* She can't help herself. Even when she's in hiding, which she has been for years now, she has to reach out, to connect, to talk about things. Meets a certain need in her. She's led a very lonely existence with limited face to face human interaction as far as we know. I thought having Daniel with her would make her less lonely."

"Which could mean he's not with her any longer," she says.

"True, but it could also mean she had other reasons for calling."

"It can't be a coincidence that she called after you looked for her in Apalach. Do you think she's there? Maybe the lead y'all were following took you very close to her and she freaked out."

"The lead was truly a dead end," I say. "Unless . . . it . . . coincidentally, randomly took us closer to her than we realized. Not the lead itself, but . . . just the area or the people or a road or a neighbor."

"Or it has nothing to do with any of that," she says. "You think she really only got as far as Apalach? Think she's in hiding just a few miles down the road from where she had been? I've been picturing her in a different country."

"Yeah, me too. And she alluded to being in a different country. I . . . wonder . . . What if she has someone there keeping an eye out? Lets her know what the police are doing or when people like me and Merrill show up."

"Or she left some sort of surveillance in place," she says. "She certainly has the technical chops for something like that."

"That's it," I say. "She knew what I was work-ing on, talked to me about Qwon's case. She's got us bugged or is hacking us. If she bugged us . . . it's probably Merrill's phone. She spent the most time around him while he was guarding Daniel and Sam.

But she probably just hacked our computer and saw
what we've been working on."

"Guarding them from the very person right
there in the house with them," Anna says, shaking her
head.

"Yeah. Says she's going to solve the Angel Diaz
case. Said if we solve it first, she'll let Daniel go—
though she indicated he might not want to leave."

"Like he's with her by choice?" Anna says.

"God, I hope not. I hope he hasn't done that to Sam.
That's been my second biggest fear—after him being
dead already."

"Yeah, mine too. I'll get our phones and computers and cars checked for bugs."

"Don't forget homes," she says. "What if she's
listening right now?"

"I seriously doubt she is," I say. "But—"

"I think just in case she is, we should give her
something to listen to," she says, closing the short gap
between us, touching and caressing and kissing me, as
she slips out of her nightgown.

Chapter Twenty-five

"I'm a little nervous about seeing everyone," Kathryn says, her blond hair blowing in the breeze.

We are standing in front of the Marina Civic Center awaiting the arrival of some of her classmates who were down here the night Angel went missing.

We've invited as many of them as we can to join us for a walk-through of the magical fateful night that Maya Angelou spoke and Kim and Ken had their house party.

"Mostly Darius," she says. "But everybody. Haven't seen most of them in almost twenty years. Never felt like I could enjoy a class reunion with Qwon sitting in prison."

I nod. "I understand."

It's early evening in Downtown Panama City, and the breeze blowing in off the bay is cool and brisk but not biting. Most of the shops are closed for the day, the streets and sidewalks nearly empty.

I'm looking forward to hearing from everyone, but especially Darius—he was not only Kathryn's boyfriend and Qwon's best friend at the time, but Qwon actually spent that night with him.

Thankfully Darius arrives first so the two of them can reconnect and exorcize any awkwardness before the others show up.

He's traded his red sport shirt with the Ace logo on it and tan trousers for a wrinkled button down and jeans. In contrast, Kathryn is wearing stylish navy slacks and a light blue blouse, only the front of which is tucked in, sexy sandals, and artisan jewelry.

Though at first they act like shy children around each other, they hug and attempt to catch up a bit.

Even all these years later, and though they are quite different—and not just because he's black and she's white, but more because his manner and dress are casual, hers more precise and put together—I can still picture them as a couple.

"I'm sorry I haven't been in touch more," Darius says. "Well, at all."

"Me too."

"I've kept up with you through Qwon. Talk to him about once a week."

"You do?"

He nods.

"That's so nice of you," she says. "Gets expensive, doesn't it?"

"What's that?"

"The collect calls."

"Oh, yeah. I don't mind. I'm always happy to hear from him."

"You're truly a good friend," she says. "Those are hard to find—particularly if you're in prison."

"You're the one he's lucky to have," Darius says.

Downtown Panama City is the soul of the city. It's old and eclectic and where most of the coolest things in the city take place. It was far better when the Fiesta and places like Panama Java and the Gallery Above were open, but it's still my favorite part of town.

Beyond the civic center where we're standing, the sun is low in the sky at the far edge of the bay. The swishing, airy sounds coming from the marina carry within swirling currents the shrieks of gulls, the slap of water against hulls, and the incessant clanging of boat ringing.

Soon the others arrive—McKenna Roberts, Amber Thurman, Billy Anderson, Rex Timberson, Derrick Edwards, Paige Askew, and at the last minute and totally unexpected, Eric Pulisfer.

All are white except for Derrick and Darius, and I wonder if their group had included just black guys or if there had been black girls in it as well.

Kathryn walks up to each one and thanks them for helping us, including Eric, who is the most surprised and the most grateful.

As soon as Kathryn accepts and welcomes Eric, the others warm to him too.

I give them a little while to reacquaint themselves and to reconnect. Like most former classmates it's not long until they are sharing memories and talking about their times.

They laugh at their fashion—the oversized tee shirts, turtlenecks, slouch socks worn over sweatpants, leggings, ballet flats, Keds, tanktops, trainers, cargo pants, camouflage, crop tops, denim, so much denim, and bangs, so many bangs, and of course high pony-tails with scrunchies or headbands—we were such dorks, weren't we? Didn't even know it. Everything came to Panama City a few years late—grunge, gla-mour, goth, preppy, Hip Hop, African, Asian.

They remember their shows—*Dawson's Creek, Cosby* (did you hear what that dirty bastard's been up to?), *Twin Peaks, The Wonder Years, Buffy, 90210, My So Called Life*—we had the best high school shows, didn't we?

The movies—*Home Alone, Titanic, Clueless, Scream, Forrest Gump, I Know What You Did Last Sum-mer*—this is sort of like that, isn't it?

I look at the too-early middle-aged group and try to picture the 90s teens they had been.

"So," I say, "we about ready to take a little walk?"

"What we're asking you to do is just say any-thing you remember from that night," Kathryn says. "Anything at all—no matter how small it may seem."

Kathryn comes across far more together, far more educated and sophisticated than the rest of the group, but she still fits in—accepts them even as they accept her.

"Maya Angelou was amazing," Amber says. "I remember feeling like happy and hopeful."

Amber has pale skin and redish-tinged blond hair. She wears no makeup, a light cotton dress, and flip flops. Not only was she with the group that night, but Kathryn actually spent the night with her after leaving downtown.

It has been a very warm February—even by North Florida standards, but I bet she'll wish she'd dressed warmer if we're still out here after the sun goes down.

"I felt the same way," McKenna says. "Haven't thought about it in so long. After what happened to Angel . . . it's easy to forget all the good things about that night."

McKenna is tall and thin with dark hair, a smattering of dark freckles on her nose and the tops of her cheeks, and thick bangs. So far she's the most talkative and energetic of the group.

"So," Kathryn says, "Maya was amazing. We came through these doors back into the world and . . ."

"Walked up Harrison Avenue," Rex says.

He's a tall, oddly shaped man in his mid-thirties with black wavy hair and a round, pale face. He's a little awkward and insecure and I picture him as a nice, girlfriendless guy on the fringe of the group back then.

"Let's do that," Kathryn says. "Just tell us what you remember."

We all start walking out of the civic center parking lot and down the sidewalk on Harrison.

"I remember seeing Angel and Qwon walking together," Amber says, her reddish hair blowing in the breeze like everybody else's. "They were up ahead of us a little. They seemed so happy. I mean, I know everyone was that night—or right when we came out of hearing Maya, but in general, they just always seemed so happy. Not all lovey-dovey but happy."

"Yeah," McKenna says, "always seemed more like good friends than a couple to me."

We pass St. Andrews Towers, cross over Beach Drive, then when nothing is coming, cross Harrison over toward where Panama Java used to be.

"Honestly," Billy Anderson says, "I thought that's what they were. I thought we all pretty much just assumed they were gay."

Billy is at least six and a half feet tall with a dark complexion, haunting green eyes, bushy hair in need of cutting beneath a misshapen ball cap, and a scraggly beard. He's got large, prominent front teeth and too much saliva, which gives a wetness to his words that is so pronounced it almost sounds like a lisp.

"Each other's beard," Derrick adds. "Each other's gay best friend."

Derrick is a trim black guy with a small head.

"Really?" Kathryn asks. "How many of you thought that?"

Everyone but Rex, Eric, Darius, and Amber raise their hands.

"We used to call them *Crying Game*," Billy says, "just like we called you and Darius and Qwon and Angel *Jungle Fever*."

A few of them laugh at the memory.

"Wow," she says. "I had no idea that was a thing anyone thought. Interesting. I'm pretty sure they were both straight." She turns to Darius. "Anything you need to tell me about my brother I don't know?"

"I think y'all were raised a certain way," he says. "Like proper. Qwon's not gay, but he . . . he was very reserved and like . . . almost the way you see religious kids be, like trying to abstain and all."

She nods. "Yeah, I think that's more it, but . . . it's interesting. Keep telling us anything you think of."

"How about questions?" Billy says, "Can we ask questions too?"

"Sure," Kathryn says.

"Have you ever been with anyone but a black guy?" he asks.

"Say it, don't spray it," Darius says. The unkind comment seems a defense for Kathryn and maybe even to give her a moment to think.

She smiles. "Why? You want to be my first white guy?"

"Shit," he says. "It's bad enough being in my goddamn mid-thirties. Sure as shit don't want to sleep with someone that age."

Everyone laughs and the group continues to bond.

"Anyone have anything real or helpful to add?" Kathryn says.

"Angel may or may not have been gay," Paige Askew says in a soft, almost apologetic voice as she speaks for the first time, "but she died a virgin."

Chapter Twenty-six

Kathryn nods. "Yeah, sadly I'm pretty sure she did. So . . . sad. I mean . . . And I don't just mean the not having sex part. That's just . . . one more thing that . . . There are no . . . words."

As if she is literally right, no one says anything for a few moments, everyone seeming to take in all over again how tragic and cruel Angel's death, Qwon's fate, and their loss has been.

Eventually, Kathryn says, "I guess we need to keep . . . going. Okay. Where'd y'all go first?"

"To my car to smoke some weed," Rex says.

"To Panama Java," McKenna says.

"Me too, "Amber says.

"Do you remember seeing Angel and Qwon there?" Kathryn asks.

They all agree they did.

We stop in front of the spot next to the Italian restaurant Ferrucci's, where Panama Java used to be. The large covered patio/courtyard is empty. Beyond it the little shop that had once been a coffee bar, then later a restaurant, and in between its basement a meth lab, now sits dark and empty—the antithesis of what it was the memorable night in January of 1999.

Merrill and I had gotten coffee and brought it out into the courtyard to one of the tables near where a female guitarist was doing an acoustic set and discussed the event we had just been to—which led into discussions on race and art and beauty and women and the world. It was truly a great night. And yet just a few feet away from us, unbeknownst to us, the lives of a small group of teenagers were about to be changed forever.

"It's so sad it's gone," Paige says. "It was a really cool place."

Her words are still soft, her demeanor shy and self-conscious, but she's talking more now and seems marginally more relaxed.

"Became a really hot place later when they started cooking meth in the basement," Billy says, his voice seeming to boom compared to Paige's.

"Where'd you go after leaving the civic center?" I ask Derrick.

"To Rex's car to smoke weed," he says. "Then we went to The Place."

"Where'd y'all get the weed?" I ask.

"Same place everybody did," Rex says. "Justice Witney."

"Was he down here that night?" I ask. "Anybody remember seeing him?"

Several of them nod.

"I bought from him that night," Derrick says.

"He was always on the periphery," Kathryn says. "But he was always around."

"I guarantee he didn't go hear any poetry be read," Billy says, his words wet, his voice whistley, "but he was down here hanging around making sales, talking shit. Sumbitch knows he likes to talk."

"Did any of you see him with or near Angel or Qwon that night?" I ask.

Most shake their heads. A few say *no*.

McKenna says, "They were at some of the same places at the same time, but I never saw them together or even speak."

"Where'd everybody go after leaving here?" Kathryn says.

About half the group went to The Place on Grace and the other half went to the Visual Arts Center.

"We're closer to the VAC from here," Kathryn says. "Want to walk there next?"

I nod.

We continue up Harrison and cross 4th Street to the Visual Arts Center, which was recently renamed Panama City Center for the Arts.

Located in a Spanish style two-story stone building with a terra-cotta roof, the building that will always be the VAC to me was once a jail, and is now an art gallery and event center.

"Most of us came here just killing time," McKenna says. "It was something to do while we waited to go to Kim and Ken's."

"I came 'cause they had wine at the reception," Billy says.

"Yeah, me too," Rex says.

"It was a cool exhibit," Amber says. "Most of the works had words in them, sort of like a marriage of poetry and painting. I really liked it."

"I liked the wine," Derrick says.

Everyone laughs.

"None of us, not the art lovers or the winos stayed long," Kathryn says. "But it was cool how they had a theme to go with what Maya had just done at the civic center."

"Did any of you see Qwon and Angel?" I ask.

"I did," McKenna says.

"Me too," Paige adds.

Several of the others join in.

"Anything stand out?" Kathryn asks.

They shake their heads.

"Not that I can recall," Billy says.

"Were they drinking the wine or had they been smoking?" I ask.

Amber shakes her head. "No. Not that you could tell."

"They were," Billy says.

"Really?" Amber asks.

"Yeah," he says, nodding, his hat moving about on his bushy hair. "Both."

"Well, I couldn't tell."

"Anyone see Justice here?" I ask.

"I did," Eric says.

It's the first time he's spoken in a while and everyone turns toward him as if they'd forgotten he was there.

"He consumed a good deal of the free wine too," he says.

Everyone waits but he doesn't add anything else.

"Okay," Kathryn says, "Shall we head over to The Place?"

We all turn and our small herd crosses Harrison and pauses at the Martin Theater.

I notice that Darius is staying close to Kathryn, even taking her arm as we cross the street.

Kathryn turns toward me and says, "We're going over to where it was, not where it is now, right?"

The Place on Grace is now just The Place and is located on Harrison on the other side of the Martin, only a single storefront between them.

"Right."

"You sure?" Billy says. "It's about dinner time. I sure could go for one of their big ass burgers."

Darius says, "Why don't we all go there for dinner together after we're done?" Though he's supposedly asking everyone, he's only looking at Kathryn.

"Cool," Billy says.

"I'm down," Derrick says.

"Sounds fun," MeKenna says. "Having our own little mini class reunion."

"Well, let's get moving," Amber says. "I missed lunch today and now y'all've got me starvin'."

We walk down the sidewalk then cut through the parking lot behind the Martin to the old mini mall where The Place once was.

Though the old building is the same, it now houses a bar, a pizza place, a coffee shop, and has a back room used for a comedy club about once a month.

Billy says, "Did you all see Qwon and Angel here? Anything stand out? Was Justice here?" His tone is light and maybe even a little mocking.

"You need to take this seriously," Eric says. "Our friend was murdered and another one of our friends has been . . . rottin' in prison for the past eighteen years and I don't think he did it."

As Eric talks, he actually takes a step toward Billy, and I wonder if perhaps Billy, who is much bigger than Eric even now, bullied him back in school.

Billy opens his mouth to say something, but Eric takes another step toward him and says, "What?"

Chapter Twenty-seven

"Sorry man," Billy says, swallowing some of the excess spit in his mouth. "Didn't mean anything by it. I'm takin' this seriously. Why I'm here. Was just playing a little 'cause I'm hungry."

"What about the answer to those questions?" Kathryn says.

"We saw Qwon and Angel here," Darius says. "By that time, we had all sort of fallen in together and were going from one place to another as a group."

She nods.

"But I don't remember seeing Justice," he says.

"He was here," Amber says. "At least at some point. I remember seeing him. Wow. I just remembered something. He was like leering at Angel when she and Qwon danced. Guess it didn't stand out 'cause he was always doing shit like that, but . . . he was really—it made me uncomfortable."

"I remember that, too," Paige says. "I always avoided him—even eye contact with him—but I always knew where he was. Tried to keep an eye on him. I remember him looking all lasciviously at her."

"Now that you say that . . . I remember Qwon stepping over to him and saying something," Derrick says. "It was real quick. Less than a minute. Didn't really think anything of it at the time, but . . . now . . . Justice left pretty soon after that."

Rex nods. "I remember that."

"I just remember how good the band was," MeKenna says, "and that everyone was starting to get buzzed from the wine at the reception, the weed, and whatever else they were sneaking out to their cars to get. The later it got, the tighter."

"I's sure as shit lit by then," Billy says.

In dress and manner Billy is more prototypically redneck than anyone else in the group, and I wonder if there were others who just weren't able to make it tonight or if he was an anomaly even back then.

"Next we went to the Fiesta," Kathryn says. "At least some of us did."

"Let's go there and split up just like y'all did that night," I say.

We walk back down Grace, cross over 4th, up through a back alley and pop out on Harrison at C&G Sporting Goods, cross the street and walk a block down to the two fantastic old buildings that once housed the best club in town.

Sitting at the corner of Beach and Harrison, The Royale Lounge is in one building and The Fiesta Room is in another, with a cool courtyard between them that feels as close to New Orleans as anything in Panama City.

We stand admiring the buildings and courtyard for a moment, mourning this fun, welcoming place that is no more, then walk around to the back.

Standing close to the back entrance, they split up into two groups—those who went into Fiesta and those who didn't.

"Of those of you who didn't," I say, "who walked down to Kim and Ken's?"

Paige raises her hand. "Angel and I walked down there together."

"See anybody on the way? Anyone mess with y'all?"

She shakes her head, but glances over at Eric.

"I didn't go in," Rex says, "but I went back to my car to smoke some more."

"I went over to the park," Derrick says. "Don't care for this place."

Eric says, "I wasn't really with this group. I came a little later. By the time I got here, everyone was dancing and carrying on, pretty drunk by then."

"We had a guy sneaking us drinks," Kathryn says. "Were all pretty wasted."

"Yeah," Eric says, "but nobody more than Qwon."

"I'd say I gave him a run for his money," Kathryn says.

"We all did," Amber says.

"He was way too fucked up to kill anybody," Billy says. "Hell, what I remember was how much he was lovin' on everybody."

"We sort of all were, weren't we?" Amber says.

"It was that kind of night," MeKenna says. "We were lit, sure, but we were also inspired by Maya and I think . . . a little nostalgic. Last year of school together. I don't know."

"It was a love fest," Kathryn says. "We were all dancing together, hugging and kissing and saying sweet things to each other. Nobody was thinking about killing anyone."

"I decided to leave after a little while," Eric says. "To be honest, I felt left out of the . . . of all the . . . of what y'all were doing. Decided to—"

"I'm sorry," Kathryn says, and steps over and hugs him.

Amber and McKenna join her and they all wrap him up in a long group hug.

In a matter of moments, he breaks down and starts crying. Soon he's sobbing.

"It's okay," Kathryn says.

"Yeah," McKenna says. "Let it out."

He cries for maybe a minute while they hold him, then begins to pull himself together as the three women let him go and step back.

"Fuckin' high school man," Billy says. "Sorry bro. I know I was a dick. Wasn't personal, but . . . I'm sorry. I really am."

"We all are," Rex says.

"I know y'all think I killed her," Eric says between sniffles, "but I didn't. I loved her. I've never hurt anyone in my whole life. I would never . . . do . . . anything . . . to . . . anyone, but especially her."

"We don't think you did," Amber says.

"I'll be honest," Billy says, "I thought you might have."

Everyone laughs. Even Eric. "I didn't kill her. I swear."

"Continue with what you were saying," I say.

"I . . . I decided to walk down to Kim and Ken's. As I was leaving, Qwon stumbled out the back door. I thought maybe he was going on down to the party too, but . . . he went around the front of the building."

"He was getting us some more goodies from the car," Billy says. "Refilling the flask. Seeing if he could find any more E."

"I came to the back door and shouted for him to grab my coat," Kathryn says. "I wanted it for when we walked down to Kim and Ken's, but he was already around the corner. So I went to the corner of the building and shouted to him. He heard me that time." She looks at Eric. "You must have already been through the parking lot and down a little ways on Beach 'cause I don't remember seeing you."

"Think I was."

"But as I turned to walk back over to the door," she says, "I saw Justice Witney on the opposite side of Beach, sort of over behind St. Andrews Towers, heading toward Kim and Ken's. He was walking very slowly and smoking. I remember that."

"Did you tell the cops?" Amber asks.

"How about Qwon's defense attorney?" McKenna says.

She nods and frowns. "It was just dismissed as a sister lying to help her brother. Same as our statements and polygraph tests and everything. I kept saying he's not my brother. Our parents just married recently. I wouldn't lie for him or anyone else I thought even might have killed Angel or anyone else."

"They kept saying we were all lying to cover up for Qwon," McKenna says. "But we weren't."

I turn to Eric. "Did you see Justice on Beach?"

He shakes his head. "I . . . but I never turned around. Never looked back. But if he was . . . that means when Angel passed me . . . she was walking directly toward him."

"What did you do?" McKenna asks.

"Angel and I said hello, exchanged a little small talk but I kept going toward the party 'cause I didn't want her to think I was following her or had just come down there to see her. When I got to the house I kept walking. I circled around to Cove then back up 4th. Took a while. By the time I got back downtown, I just decided to go home."

"And whatever happened to Angel probably had already," Kathryn says.

"I should've walked her back up here." Eric says.

"Did she say where she was headed?" Kathryn asks.

"Said she was bored, tired of just standing around waiting, wanted to get her coat anyway and would probably just wait up there for y'all or see if she could sneak in Fiesta. Said she'd see me back at the party later and maybe we could dance together if I wanted to. She was always so decent to me. So kind.

Those were the last words she ever said to me, the last time I ever saw her."

Kathryn shakes her head. "I waited by the back door for Qwon to come back with my jacket, just getting some fresh air. The smoke was always like a thick fog in Fiesta. I almost started to walk on down to the party, but Qwon was back so quick and . . . Darius was still inside and we were having so much fun. If we had all just left a little sooner. Justice was down there on that dark street with Angel. Just the two of them."

"But wait," Derrick says. "When I walked from the park to Kim and Ken's, I saw you at the back door."

Kathryn nods. "I remember you waving."

"I walked straight down Beach to Kim and Ken's and . . . I didn't see Justice. Saw Angel, but not him."

"Really?"

"Had to be within a few minutes," Derrick adds, "or even less of Eric, Justice, and Angel all being on Beach and I only saw Angel."

"He must've been hiding," Billy says. "Waiting there in the shadows to pounce and rape and kill our friend. You could've walked within a few feet of him and not even known."

"Seems like I would've heard something," he says, "but . . . wow, what if I did? I wish I had known, wish to God I heard something. I would have . . . fucked him up."

"Can't believe while all that was going on all I could do was think how much I wanted one more dance with Qwon," Amber says. "Grabbed him as soon as he came in the door. We just didn't know Angel was in such . . . we had no idea. If we had, of course we would've been down there protecting her."

"Not that she ever seemed like she needed protecting," Rex says.

"No wonder Justice knew everything to say to the cops to set up Qwon," McKenna says. "He did it. He knew everything."

"Of course he did," Billy says. "We knew Qwon couldn't've done it. He was back inside with us. Had been gone less than like eight minutes. We were all drinking and dancing again while that motherfucker was killin' her."

Chapter Twenty-eight

Billy having convinced us that we could discuss the rest of the evening in the warmth and comfort of The Place while eating cheeseburgers, we are now seated around a long rectangular table in the back near the stage.

On the stage, in a rare weeknight performance, local musician Aaron Bearden is performing an acoustic set of originals. Ordinarily he plays guitar and sings with two bands in town, Turtlefoot and 4th Street, but it's just him tonight, and he tells us during his first break that he's rehearsing new music he's about to take on the road with a bassist and drummer from indie bands we should recognize but don't.

Acoustic sets are my favorite and the one he's playing is particularly good, the lyrics smart, literate, and touching, and it reminds me of Jason Isbell and early Gin Blossoms. Aaron's music makes for a nice backdrop to our conversation.

McKenna says, "Where the hell'd our lives go and what did we do with them?"

"I've done exactly shit with mine," Billy says.

"Don't feel like I've done much," Derrick says. "Especially given how much time I've had."

"What life?" Kathryn says. "I have no life."

"You kidding?" McKenna says. "You're the only one who's actually done something with your life. You dedicated yours to something real, a cause, something greater than a sad, selfish little existence."

"I propose a toast," Amber says, raising her glass of beer. "To Kathryn, who after all this time is still fighting the good fight. The very definition of devotion, faithfulness, love, and seeking justice. To Kathryn."

"To Kathryn," we all say.

Glasses clink. Sips are taken.

"Not many people would've have done what you've done," McKenna says.

"Not many *could* have," Darius says. "Qwon is lucky to have you and we're honored to know you."

Kathryn is visibly touched but also clearly embarrassed. "Thank you," she says to Darius, and I wonder if there's not a little something rekindling inside them both. "Thank you all, but the truth is . . . I haven't accomplished anything yet. All my efforts. All this time. Nothing has come of it so far, but I'm really hopeful something will now, so thank you all for helping us tonight. Now let's get back to the case, okay?"

"*Okay*," Billy says, as if a child acquiescing to a parent. "Yes, ma'am."

"So we all sort of stumble down Beach to Kim and Ken's," Kathryn is saying, "and when we get there and start looking for Angel and find out she's not there, a couple of us go looking for her. Me, Qwon, Darius—"

"And me," McKenna says.

"We were not in the best of shape to be searching for anyone," Darius says. "Could hardly walk."

"True, but . . . we had to," Kathryn says.

"We didn't see her or Justice or—" he glances at Eric—"or anyone."

"We all looked around for a while, but didn't see her," Kathryn says.

"When they didn't come back right away," Amber says, "a few more of us went to help."

"And when they didn't come back for a while," Derrick says, "pretty much the rest of us went."

"So we're all like looking for her," McKenna says, "until someone says her car is gone and we realized she just went home—took off like she had so many times before."

"Except she hadn't," Kathryn says.

"But we didn't know," Amber says. "We thought she had so we just . . . went back to the party."

"Qwon and Angel were on her car that night," Kathryn says. "It was better than his. He had a clunker but he had a cellphone."

"That's the thing to remember," Darius says. "Not many of us had those at that time. It's not like we stayed in touch back then the way we do now. Just wasn't a thing."

"It's not like Qwon could call her house," Kathryn says. "And he had done that same thing so many times before, so . . ."

"If they were on her car together," I say, "she just left Qwon."

"She knew we'd give him a ride," Darius says. "He was staying at my house that night anyway."

Something occurs to me and I sit up a bit.

"Do any of you know who drove them down that night?" I ask. "Qwon or Angel."

"He did," Darius says. "Saw them pull up. Why?"

"Did he lock the car?"

He nods. "Always."

"And he still had the keys when y'all were at Fiesta," I say, "because he went out to the car to refill and whatnot."

"Yeah?" Darius says.

Kathryn's eyes widen. "I see what you're saying. He had the keys. Not her. So why did we think she had left without him? She couldn't have. But it didn't occur to our drunk asses that night. Damn."

"It's that," I say, "sure, but . . . it's also . . . when the car was found . . . there was no sign of forced entry. It wasn't broken into or hot-wired."

"Oh shit," Derrick says. "Only Qwon could've opened it. Does that mean he really did it?"

"Wait," Kathryn says. "He didn't. He couldn't have. So . . . there's . . . Something's not right. It could've been unlocked."

"That would get her in but wouldn't get it cranked," I say. "It's possible she had keys too. Maybe he had the spare and she always carried hers, but . . ."

"I wish he was here so we could ask him," Kathryn says. "I'm tellin' you there's no way he could have done it. It's just not possible."

I nod. "Tell you what. Give me a minute. I'll call the prison and ask him."

"You can do that?" McKenna says.

"Be right back," I say.

I walk out the back door and stand on the platform at the top of the stairs and call the institution.

It's dark now and cooler, but it's a nice night and downtown is peaceful and quiet.

It takes a little while, but with the help of the control room sergeant and the officer on duty in the infirmary, I get Qwon on the phone.

"How're you feeling?" I ask.

"Better. Thanks."

"Got a couple of questions for you," I say, "and I need you to be as honest as you can."

"Have been with you about everything," he says. "Got nothin' to hide. Not afraid of the truth."

"How did you get downtown the night of the Maya Angelou reading and Kim and Ken's house party?"

"We took her car. Usually did. It was better than mine."

"Who drove?"

"I did."

"Did you have your own keys or did you use hers?"

"Hers."

"Did you lock the car?"

"Yes, sir. Always."

"So when you went out to it from the Fiesta . . ."

"I had to unlock it."

"Did you lock it back?" I ask.

"Yes, sir. I did. Alwa—"

"So if you had the keys how did she leave? Or how did the killer move her car?"

"I have no idea," he says. "I honestly don't. I was real drunk that night. Wasn't thinkin' straight. Didn't even occur to me at first. Later when it did, when I was like, 'Wait, I've got the keys, how'd she leave,' I checked my pocket and they were gone. Then I was like . . . 'Did she come by and get them from me and I didn't remember?' That's how messed up I was that night. Later, like the next day or something, I thought maybe her killer lifted them from me without me even knowin'. You know in all this time no one's ever asked about that, about the keys or how the killer got them. I would've been happy to answer the questions about them on the polygraph. Still am. I just have no idea what happened to the keys. I know it makes me look guilty, but . . . I'm tellin' the truth— just like I have about everything."

Back inside, I tell the others what he said.

"Doesn't look good for him, does it?" Eric says.

"Wouldn't he just make up something about them?" Billy says. "He could lie about her having a set or leaving them in the car."

"Wait," Kathryn says. "What if that's it? What if he was so out of it, he left them in the car? What if he just thought he locked it and took the keys back with him, but what if he left them? What if Angel's killer was going to break in and hot wire it but found out he didn't have to?"

"Why would her killer take her car at all?" Rex asks. "Why not take his own car? Why mess with hers?"

It's a good question and I can think of a few answers—the most obvious being that it was Qwon who killed her. The other being whoever it was knew her well enough to know that if they moved her car, everyone would think she left on her own—like she had so many times before.

"But Qwon couldn't have done it," Amber says. She looks at Kathryn. "He was still at the party when we left, wasn't he?"

Kathryn nods. "We left pretty early. We just weren't really feeling it."

"Y'all left a good hour or more before we did," Darius says.

Kathryn says, "Qwon stayed the night with Darius and I stayed the night with Amber."

I nod.

"So here's the thing," Amber says. "Qwon is still at the party when we leave, hasn't been out of anyone's sight the entire time we've been downtown, stays an hour or more after we leave . . . and yet when we pass by Angel's house, which wasn't far from downtown and was only a few blocks from mine . . . her car was in her driveway."

"It was?"

"Yes," Amber says.

Kathryn nods. "It was."

"Do you think she was dead by that point?" Amber says. "It's all so crazy. At that point we thought she was fine. Went home. Crashed. We had done so much drinking and dancing and . . . other stuff. Kathryn got the call that she was missing before I even woke up the next morning and went out searching for her immediately. But she was already dead when we passed her car on the way home earlier that night, right?"

I shrug.

"Could've been."

"I just don't see how her car got back to her house. Did she drive it? Was she killed after that?"

Chapter Twenty-nine

Anna calls me as I'm driving home and tells me with obvious excitement in her voice that she thinks she's just had a major breakthrough in the case.

She's as upbeat and genuinely thrilled as I've heard her in a long time, and I'm happy not only for her brilliant help but the collateral joy it's bringing her.

But by the time I get home she is crying and shaking, too upset to talk at first.

"Take your time," I say. "Come sit down and let's talk about it."

I lead her to our library/study in the back of the house—what was originally designed to be the formal living room—so we could have privacy and be alone. Even though Sam's asleep in her hospital bed in the living room, it's not the same as it truly being just the two of us.

As we walk down the hallway, I wonder if something has happened to Johanna, though I spoke to her earlier in the evening and she was fine, or Dad, who's undergoing treatment for chronic lymphocytic leukemia, or Daniel—though in each case I think I'd be the one to get the call. Maybe it's something to do with her parents.

I feel my way through the dark library and turn on a floor lamp in the corner, then lead her over to the old brown love seat that had been my dad's mom's.

For a long moment I just hold her, her head on my chest, her crying softly, tears damping my shirt.

"Take your time," I say. "And know whatever it is, we'll face it together, figure it out. No matter what."

The books that once were mostly stacked on the floor of my old trailer in the Prairie Palm now line floor-to-ceiling shelves in this beautiful book room that holds everything from my earliest theology and criminology texts to books about the Shroud of Turin, the Atlanta Child Murders, the poetry of Rumi, and the most recent Paul Auster novel I purchased.

Eventually, Anna lifts her head, leans back a little and turns toward me and says, "Chris called."

I nod. I should've guessed that's what it was.

"Said he'd be out in just a few days. *A few days.* He was so arrogant and . . . just like he used to be. And . . . I . . . I got physically ill. Actually threw up. I kept thinking . . . he's going to be part of Taylor's life, part of our lives . . . forever. Always causing us problems or trying to kill us or get custody of Taylor. That's what he said—well, one of many things he said—he plans to fight for full custody of Taylor. Going to claim that we set him up and subjected him to all sorts of horrors in prison, that you used your influence inside to have him tortured and raped and . . . said his attorney was already working on civil suit against you and he hopes to be able to convince the state's attorney to file criminal charges as well. Said his mission in life is to get his daughter away from us and make our lives as miserable as possible."

I reach up and wipe the tears from her cheeks. "It's going to be okay. *We're* going to be okay."

"I know how he is," she says. "How ruthless. How relentless."

"I know how we are," I say. "How strong. How resilient."

She smiles and kisses me. "I know, but . . . he fights dirty. He . . . I won't let him get Taylor. He'll . . . Can you imagine what he'd . . . the effect he'd have on her. He's not going to . . . I'll kill him first."

"Hey, it's not going to come to that," I say. "We're going to be okay. We'll protect Taylor and—"

"We can't afford the kind of attorney we need to fight him," she says. "We're barely making it now, and with you quitting the prison . . . and us trying to take care of Sam . . ."

"Just find the attorney we need," I say, "I'll find the money to pay him."

"Where? How?"

"Listen to me," I say. "I promise you . . . we're going to protect Taylor and each other and Johanna and everyone else. Don't let him get in your head. Don't let him trick you into thinking he's more power-ful or capable than he is. We'll do what we have to. Okay? You know that. We'll move back into my little trailer in Pottersville if we have to. We'll do whatever it takes."

"He said when he gets out he's moving to Wewa," she says.

I nod. "Good. That'll make it easier."

"Make what easier?"

"Keeping an eye on him. Dealing with his—with him. First thing tomorrow find the attorney you want and I'll find the money. We'll start there."

"Thank you."

I have no idea where or how I'll find the kind of money we'll need, but . . . I'll think about that tomorrow—or later tonight when I can't sleep. Not now.

"I love you," I say.

"Sorry about all this," she says. "Sorry I came with so much baggage. Are you regretting getting together with me yet? Do you want to . . . we haven't made it official. You can still—"

I put a finger to her lips as I push off the couch, turn, and kneel before her.

Pulling out the small box from my pocket, I say, "Anna, I've loved you my entire life, and it seems like I've waited for you about that long. There's an awful lot that is wrong in this world, but one thing that is absolutely right is us. I love you with every cell of my body, every bit of my soul, every second of my life. I'm so grateful that we're together and I will never, not for one moment, take that for granted. Ever. In my heart and everywhere it matters most, you are already my wife, but will you do me the honor of making it official? Will you marry me?"

"I already have," she says. "I will again. Officially. Unofficially. Over and over again. Yes. Yes. Yes."

I remove the ring from the box and place it on her long, elegant finger.

I had found it at an antique store in downtown Panama City before meeting Kathryn and the others, and had planned to wait for the perfect time to propose again, not knowing it would arrive so soon.

She gasps. "It's so beautiful. I love it. I love you."

She holds her hand out and up and admires her new ring. "Wow, I didn't realize how much I need a manicure."

Her hard working hands not only care for Taylor and Johanna and me, but Sam, who was a stranger to her not so long ago. Her hands are beautiful and strong and I tell her so.

"That extraordinary and truly exquisite ring is unworthy of your perfect and breathtakingly beautiful hands."

Our eyes lock and she looks at me in that way—the way everyone should be looked at at least once in their lives, and the way I'm fortunate enough to be looked at every day.

After a long moment of us exchanging that which is unutterable—as Rumi said, *Silence is the language of God, all else is poor translation*—she leans down and gets on the floor with me, and we kiss.

Joyful tears have joined the ones of dread and painful memories on her cheeks from before and they dampen my face as we kiss, then my body a little later as we make love for the first time as an officially engaged couple on the floor of our library.

The library, like our home and children and each other, is sacred to us, and if Chris Taunton thinks he has any chance at all of profaning or defiling or destroying any of it, he's truly incredibly enormously mistaken—something I plan to point out to him hard enough to make a lasting impression.

Chapter Thirty

Later, much later, after we've made love and looked at her ring a lot and hugged and kissed and held and comforted, we are sitting on our bed with the case notes spread out before us.

"After you hear what I have to say," she says, "you'll be even happier you proposed to me."

"Not possible."

"So sweet," she says, leaning over to kiss me. "You make me so happy. I love my ring. I love you. Can't believe how awful I felt earlier and how wonderful I feel now. I know Chris is going to be a . . . but I feel hopeful again . . . and I'm just so damned happy. Who knew a ring on my finger could make such a difference?"

"I'm just glad it did."

"Thank you for asking," she says.

"Thank you for saying yes."

"Anytime. Every time."

She looks back down at the papers in front of her, moves a few around finds what she's looking for, then puts the rest back in the folder. "Okay, you ready for this?"

"I am."

"Two things and two things only give Justice Witney's testimony any credibility at all," she says.

"That he knew where the car was and that the cell-phone tower evidence backed up his story."

I nod.

"Without those there's nothing," she says, "only his word against Qwon's. No actual, tangible evidence."

"Exactly."

"What if I told you I can explain away both?"

"Really?"

"Really," she says. "Aren't I a great wife?"

"The best."

"Let's start with the car," she says. "Guess whose stepdad worked at the airport and who helped him part time?"

"Ah . . . let's see . . . How many guesses do I get?"

"Justice's stepdad did some general caretaking and light maintenance," she says. "Name is Carrie Gardner, Jr. Young Witney worked with him on the weekends. One of their jobs was to blow off the parking lot, keep an eye on the cars, and report any that appeared abandoned."

"Wow."

"Because the stepdad had a different name . . . defense investigator just missed this. Cops may have too, but even if they didn't, it was in their best interest that it not come out—just like the identity of the Crime Stoppers tipster. I think Witney just happened to see Angel's car out there. Knew the cops were looking for it. Sat on it until he needed it. Used it when it suited him."

"Brilliant work," I say. "Really fantastic. Thank you for—"

"You're bragging on me extra because you're about to say the prosecution would argue that the fact that he worked there part-time just means he was familiar with it and would have suggested it to Qwon as a place to dump the car. You were, weren't you?"

I smile. "It is brilliant work. I mean it. It's incredible. And of course the prosecution is going to argue that. Doesn't change how valuable what you've uncovered is or that it could have happened just like you say. Probably did."

"No *probably* to it. It *did*. And what I'm about to tell you next proves it."

"Well, let's hear it."

"You know how everyone keeps saying that the cellphone tower evidence fits Justice's story?"

"Yeah?"

"Well, it's just the opposite," she says. Justice kept changing his story to fit the cellphone evidence. Look at this."

She hands me a transcript of Justice's first interview. Several passages are highlighted.

I glance over them.

"In his first interview he knows very little," she says. "And that's after they've met with him for several hours before they started recording. No telling what all the told him during that time. But notice how many things he doesn't mention. He doesn't say anything about going to St. Andrews or back downtown to get Qwon's jacket and phone or to Coram's later when they finish."

I look over his statement. She's right.

"Why did he say more later?" she says. "Because the investigators got the cellphone records. And they needed to explain why Justice was where he was and Qwon was where he was. They have to have a statement that matches the records so it has credibility, so they say 'Your phone says you were here during this time and Qwon's says he was there. How can you explain that? What were you doing here at this time?' Et cetera."

"You're saying the Bay County Sheriff's Investigators . . ."

"Believed the black boyfriend was guilty," she says, "and worked with the only witness they had to prove it. You can even see in the second interview where they had wrong information about where a certain cell tower was, so Justice says he and Qwon went to McDonald's on 15th Street, but by the third interview when they realized the tower was in a different location, he changed his story to say they went to St. Andrews to get weed. Look at what he says."

I do, reading the passages she's highlighted in the second and third interviews. She's right about what Justice says, how he changes his story, and she may just be right about what it means.

"Why would they go to McDonald's before they burn the body and then Coram's right after?" she says. "And notice he doesn't even mention going to Coram's until the final interview. Also, Justice is a drug dealer. He was downtown supplying all the kids all night. He had weed. He certainly didn't have to go buy some from another dealer. But they had to explain why there was a ping to his phone from that tower and that's what he came up with. He also had to explain why Qwon's phone showed he was downtown and not with Justice, so he had to make up the story about Qwon leaving his jacket and phone and them having to go back for it. Qwon wasn't with him. He was downtown like Kathryn and all the others said. So Justice makes up this bullshit story about Qwon leaving his jacket and phone where he killed Angel and them having to go back down and get it."

I read some more of Justice's statements.

"It's not just that his story changes," she says. "It's the way it changes. It's how it evolves—but only evolves based on info the investigators have. They realize that Qwon's phone pinged off the Bayou George tower later that night and they had to account for it. Do you know why it did? Because he spent the night with Darius. That's where Darius lived. But since they've got to account for it, they have Justice say that he and Qwon went for pancakes in the middle of the night after having cremated Angel's remains. But look at this."

She hands me the cell tower records and points to places where she's highlighted.

"Isn't it interesting the places where Qwon's phone pings off a tower versus Justice's? Except for when they're downtown, they're never together. That's how you know it's bullshit. Completely fabricated.

The Coram's Bayou George tower ping is just Qwon's phone. Justice wasn't there. St. Andrews was just Justice's. Qwon wasn't there. Now listen to his final statement. See how much it has evolved and how much they're leading him. Hell, he even apologizes to them when he leaves something out they wanted him to say."

She opens her laptop and plays the file of the audio recording of Justice's final interview.

"Yes, sir, I did. I's like nigga did you find her? He said 'Wait 'til you see this shit.' He drove out of downtown, down Beach . . . toward like St. Andrews, but stops at one of those little pullover places where white people park to look at the bay. We get out, go around to the back of the car and he's like 'Wait for it . . . wait for it . . . look at this shit.' Then he pops the trunk and . . . and . . . Angel's dead body is laying there all folded up unnaturally and shit. Motherfucker was all like, 'No bitch gonna breakup with or blackmail me. Look at that. All these little niggas runnin' around hard with their nines and their Tupac bandanas thinkin' they street and shit. Not a one of 'em ever put a bitch down.' I was like why you showin' me this shit? 'Cause nigga, you gonna help me deal with this bitch's body.' I's like hell no I ain't. 'Hells yes you are. I know shit on you, Just. Plus your prints and hair and fibers and shit are in her car now.' Then the nigga pulls out a camera and snaps a picture of me standing there beside her dead body. 'You stirred up in this shit now,' he says. 'Question is, you wants to be stirred up to the top or not?'"

"So that's why you agreed to help him get rid of the body?"

"Yes, sir. Didn't have a choice. Knew everyone would believe his little goody-goody ass over my drug-dealing one."

"Why do you think he came to you?"

"'Couple a reasons. One, I the most criminal element, street nigga he know. And two, he know my uncle owns Legacy."

"And what is Legacy?"

"Affordable direct cremation for cheap ass niggas don't want to be buried."

"Did he say that?"

"He said a lot of shit. But yeah. He was like, 'We can burn her, bro. No one'll ever know.'"

"So that's what y'all did, cremated her?"

"Eventually. First, I was like if I'm gonna do this shit, I gots to be high. So we drove over to St. Andrews to one of my boys. Got hooked up."

"You got high?"

"We got fucked up. Everything after that's a little you know fuzzy and shit, but . . ."

"Then what'd you do?"

"Ah, let's see. Then we's headed over to Legacy and Qwon was like, I left my phone and my jacket where I killed her, we got to go get it. I's like, nigga we ridin' around in the bitche's car with her dead body in the trunk and you want to go back downtown where everybody lookin' for her?"

"So you drove back downtown?"

"Part of the way, then we parked and walked the rest of it."

"Did you ask him where and how he killed her?"

"Yeah. Nigga wasn't real specific. Said he'd been look-ing for her and got tired. Sat his ass down on one of those benches on Beach Drive that looks out over the bay. She pull up in her car and said get in. Need to talk to you. He was like, everybody's looking for you. But he got in. Left his jacket on the bench. The phone was in it. Said he had gotten hot and took it off to take a piss. Said she drove to some dark, secluded spot over behind or beside the civic center and parked. He thought they were about to fuck, but she said she was gettin' back with her ex."

"Eric Pulsifer?"

"Yeah. Said he was like, 'What the fuck?' They started arguing and fighting. She told him he wasn't gonna make trou-ble for her or mess with Eric 'cause she knew too much shit on him and could turn him into the cops. Also told him she knew he'd been cheatin' on her and guess what, two can play at that. Told him she's already fucked ol' Pulsifer while he was hangin' with the fags at the Fiesta. Think she hinted that she thought he might be gay. Said he lost it and started beating her ass. Said some shit like she taunted and mocked him. Said he hit like a girl. She was a tough bitch, promise you that. Said she started calling him names and making fun of the size of his dick. Said she thought black guys were supposed to be big, but she could never even feel his little limp dick, even when he gave her all three inches as hard as he could. He said he snapped and lost it and before he realized what he was doing, he was on top of her, his hands around her throat, chokin' her, stranglin' the shit out of her, watching the defiance, then fear, then panic, then realiza-tion in her eyes, then seein' the life go out of them. Kept sayin' over and over he was glad he did it. He'd do it again. How cool it was to see the life leave her big dark eyes. Then he threw her *ass in the trunk and drove around trying to think of what to do next—and thought of my black ass and my uncle's crematorium."*

"When y'all went back down to get Qwon's jacket, did y'all see anybody?"

"Lots of people. All still lookin' for Angel. Not knowin' they's lookin' at the fuckin' angel of death right there in the nigga standin' beside me. We acted like we's still lookin' for her just like they was. I remember someone said 'aren't you cold' to Qwon but can't remember who it was. We pretended to look. He got his jacket. Checked his phone. Had a lot of missed calls. Think he made a few calls. Pretended to look for Angel some more, then someone notice her car was gone and said ah shit bitch just went home, so they went to the party and we walked back to where we'd hid her car and drove over to Legacy."

"And cremated Angel?"

"Yes, sir. Snuck in there late that night. Did the deed."

"What did you do with her ashes?"

"Gave 'em to him. Cleaned out the crematorium. Made sure there were no teeth or bone fragments or any shit like that, gave him the ashes, and got the hell out of there. Have no idea what he did with her remains after that. Said he was gonna make sure to scatter them where no one would ever find them."

"What happened next?"

"After all this, after all I'd done for this nigga he was like, 'I'm hungry. Let's go get some chicken and waffles.' I was like how the hell can you eat? That's some cold shit. I was like fuck no, nigga, I ain't goin' to eat no goddamn waffles after just burnin' a bitch. He was like 'Nigga, I own your ass now. If I say we goin' to eat, we goin' to eat. If I say you payin', you

payin'.' So three o'clock in the morning, we drive up 231 to Coram's in Bayou George and I sat there and watched while that cold ass nigga ate fuckin' chicken and waffles."

"Were you still on Angel's car?"

"Oh, ah, no, sir. Sorry. Forgot that. We's on his. When we went back downtown to get his jacket, we got his car too. I drove it. I was like I ain't driving the car with the body in the back."

"So you had two cars at Legacy?"

"Yes, sir."

"And when you left Legacy?"

"He drove her car and I drove his. He went and hid her car and I followed and picked him up."

"So you can take us to Angel's car?"

"Yes, sir."

"You know where it is?"

"Yes, sir."

"And you're willing to take us there?"

"Yes, sir. I am."

Chapter Thirty-one

I fall asleep—or fail to—reading the transcripts of the polygraphs from the case and wondering how to best deal with Chris.

He's going to be a problem, an open sore of irritation and aggravation, of harassment and provocation, for the rest of our lives—or at least the rest of his, and I'm not exactly sure what to do about him. I do know he represents a real threat to the peace, happiness, and tranquility of our lives.

The polygraphs are a nice distraction.

After a few control questions, each witness was asked the same questions.

Examiner: Were you with Acqwon Lewis on the night of January 16, 1999 between the hours of 6:00 p.m. and 2:00 a.m.?

Darius: Yes.

Examiner: Did he ever leave your sight for more than a few minutes?

Darius: No.

Examiner: Did Acqwon Lewis kill Angel Diaz?

Darius: No. There's no way he could have. He was with me all night.

Examiner: Please just answer yes or no. Did Acqwon Lewis kill Angel Diaz?

Darius: No.

Examiner: Were you with Acqwon Lewis on the night of January 16, 1999 between the hours of 6:00 p.m. and 2:00 a.m.?

Billy: Yes.

Examiner: Did he ever leave your sight for more than a few minutes?

Billy: No.

Examiner: Did Acqwon Lewis kill Angel Diaz?

Billy: No.

Examiner: Were you with Acqwon Lewis on the night of January 16, 1999 between the hours of 6:00 p.m. and 2:00 a.m.?

McKenna: Yes.

Examiner: Did he ever leave your sight for more than a few minutes?

McKenna: No.

Examiner: Did Acqwon Lewis kill Angel Diaz?

McKenna: No.

Examiner: Were you with Acqwon Lewis on the night of January 16, 1999 between the hours of 6:00 p.m. and 2:00 a.m.?

Kathryn: Yes.

Examiner: Did he ever leave your sight for more than a few minutes?

Kathryn: No.

Examiner: Did Acqwon Lewis kill Angel Diaz?

Kathryn: No.

Examiner: Were you with Acqwon Lewis on the night of January 16, 1999 between the hours of 6:00 p.m. and 2:00 a.m.?

Amber: Yes.

Examiner: Did he ever leave your sight for more than a few minutes?

Amber: No.

Examiner: Did Acqwon Lewis kill Angel Diaz?

Amber: No.

There are pages and pages of these. All the same. All about useless for my purposes. The defense team was responsible for these and had a very narrow focus—with one goal in mind, bolstering Aqwon's defense. Since the tests weren't admissible in court, the strategy seems to be to either use them to get the investigators to look at other suspects besides Qwon or, failing that, use them in the media to sway public opinion.

Perhaps the most notable aspect of the exercise besides the limited scope of the questions is who's not tested—Eric, Justice, Zelda, Paige, Derrick, and others.

Qwon's tests take up many more pages—and not only because there are three tests but because there are so many questions.

Unlike the witnesses, only one of Qwon's was initiated by the defense team. The other two were conducted by the police and sheriff's departments.

Examiner: Is your name Acqwon Jefferson Lewis?

Acqwon: Yes.

Examiner: Are you a senior at Bay High School?

Acqwon: Yes.

Examiner: Are you a drug dealer?

Acqwon: No.

Examiner: Do you live in Panama City, Florida?

Acqwon: Yes.

Examiner: Do you like ice cream?

Acqwon: Yes.

Examiner: Do you have your own cellphone?

Acqwon: Yes.

Examiner: Is Ronald Regan the current president of the United States?

Acqwon: No.

Examiner: Have you ever lied?

Acqwon: Yes.

Examiner: Are you lying now?

Acqwon: No.

Examiner: Have you ever cheated on a test in school?

Acqwon: No.

Examiner: Did you kill Angel Diaz?

Acqwon: No. Absolutely not.

Examiner: Answer with either a *yes* or a *no* only. Did you kill Angel Diaz?

Acqwon: No.

Examiner: Do you know who killed Angel Diaz?

Acqwon: No.

Chapter Thirty-two

"Sometimes I think maybe I *did* kill her," Qwon is saying.

"Really?"

Unable to sleep and not wanting to lie awake and obsess over the nightmare we're about to experience of Chris Taunton coming back into our lives, I slipped out of bed, dressed, and drove to the prison to talk to Qwon.

Placed in confinement again by Sergeant Troy Payne, his isolation and the late hour have him both contemplative and talkative.

I'm seated in the hallway next to the solid steel door. He's seated inside the cell next to the door. The food slot is open and we're communicating through it.

"I keep wondering if it's . . . if I'm dreaming . . . if it's a nightmare . . . or if it really happened."

"You don't know?"

"Thing is . . . I don't think I could kill anyone."

His voice is night dry and thick with sleep.

"Like I'm just not capable," he continues. "But I don't remember much about that night after a certain point because I was . . . wasted. I drank way, way too much. And I took some . . . I don't know, ecstasy or something. I remember feeling so good, being all in love—with life, with the world, with my friends, everybody. Then I remember feeling so bad. Worst ever."

"Just tell me what you remember."

"I don't even care anymore," he says. "I mean about what happens to me or . . . what I mean is, I want to know the truth. Don't care what it is. And if I somehow did it, I want to know. But I really want to know. Want to remember it, remember how I felt and exactly what I did and why. No wondering. No guessing. No tryin' to fill in the gaps with . . ."

I start to say something, but he continues.

"When I think back I—and this is every time I ever think back to that night—I feel so guilty. I have these flashes of . . . I don't know if they're memories or like imaginings. I remember her walking away and letting her go. Remember thinkin' I should go with her or try to sneak her in. Something. Guilt just comes. Floods me. I feel selfish and sad, but also happy then angry. I remember dancing like . . . it was like I was at a rave—like what I picture a rave being like, you know? House music blasting, everybody jumping up and down to the monotonous pounding of the beat. I remember kissing strangers, making out with an ex-girlfriend, and . . . kissing a guy. Or maybe he kissed me. Did I go in the dressing room? Is that where it happened? Maybe it wasn't an ex-girlfriend. Maybe it was an old friend dressed like a girl. All the sequins and makeup, the wig and those sexy ass high heel boots and the smell of stripper perfume. Am I a gay? Did I kill her because I felt so . . . Did she . . .

Maybe she came in and saw me somehow. Maybe she made a scene, called me a faggot and I killed her."

If anything like that would've happened, witnesses—and not just the ones from his friend group—would've reported it. At least some of what he's saying didn't happen. Did any of it?

"Were you attracted to your friend who was in the drag show that night? I ask.

He shakes his head. "I really like her, and I have no problem with him being gay or her being a woman now—she transitioned a few years back—but no, I'm not. I wasn't attracted to him back then or her now."

"So you keep in touch?"

"Not many people do," he says. "She does."

"You've been in prison for a long, long time," I say. "All your adult life. Have you been sexually active?"

"You asking if I've fucked or been fucked by men since I've been in? You think I'm a—"

"I'm wondering if that might be what has you imagining some of this."

"Oh. No. I've never had sex with anyone in here. 'Cept myself."

This is a different Qwon. Different demeanor. Different attitude. Different way of talking—not only his language, but his delivery. There's an edge to everything he says and does. Am I seeing a side of him that's always been there? Did this Qwon kill Angel? Or is this the result of not enough sleep, too much isolation, and grief and guilt induced nightmares?

"I don't think I could kill anyone," he says. "So why do I wonder if I did?"

"I'm not sure."

"If I didn't . . . If all or most of this is just bad dreams and guilty imaginings . . . where is it coming from?"

I shrug, but don't say anything. Instead, try to give him time to see if any answers emerge.

"Wait," he says, sitting up. "Wait just a—Why do I think Justice hit on me or hinted at wanting us to . . . I think he maybe made a pass at me and I . . . I guess I ignored it. I'm not sure I even realized what it was at the time. Guess I hoped I was wrong. Wait. Did he try to kiss me? Did he kiss me and I shut him down? Is that why he—did he do all this to me because I rejected him?"

Chapter Thirty-three

The next morning when I walk out in the living room to check on Sam, Merrill is sitting beside her bed, holding her hand and whispering to her.

"Morning," I say.

"I brought breakfast," he says. "And big news." Anna walks in behind me, holds her ring hand up, and says, "We have some big news of our own."

As I drift toward the kitchen table to start putting the food on plates, she goes over and shows Merrill and Sam her ring.

"Isn't it beautiful?" she says to Sam. "Do you like it?"

"This shit's been a fuckin' lifetime in the making," Merrill says.

"And absolutely worth the wait," Anna says, then to Sam, "You hungry? Let's get you sitting up and get some breakfast in you."

Merrill steps into the kitchen and shakes my hand. "*Mazel tov.*"

"Thanks."

I put on coffee and Merrill and I get breakfast ready while Anna feeds Sam. Eventually, Anna, Merrill, and I wind up at our table eating breakfast.

I notice Anna is eating quickly, and realize she's probably trying to finish before Taylor wakes up. She's already slept longer than she normally does.

"Did you get called out last night?" Anna asks me. "Or did I just dream that?"

"Couldn't sleep," I say. "Drove out to the prison to talk to Qwon."

"In the middle of the night?"

I nod. "Wish I could interview every suspect and witness in the middle of the night."

"I bet," she says.

We are quiet, all of us eating.

"So," she says to Merrill, "what's your big news?"

"I know why Justice Witney was such an eager beaver witness for the prosecution and why he gladly did his little six month stint in the joint for the part he played in the coverup."

"Eager beaver?" I say.

He shrugs.

"Why?" she says. "Tell us. And talk fast."

"He'd already been arrested earlier," he says. "Was looking at attempted murder and some serious drug trafficking charges."

"Before Angel went missing?" I say.

"November of the previous year."

"So he was already talkin' to the police," Anna says. "But why didn't the defense know about it? Or his classmates? How was he back in school? It shouldn't've been sealed. He wasn't a minor."

"Was in November when his ass got arrested," he says. "Turns out ol' Justice has the same birthday as our lord and savior."

"Those dirty bastards," Anna says.

"Jesus and Justice?" Merrill says.

"No. The prosecutors. Even though he had been a minor when he was arrested if he was benefitting in that case by testifying in Qwon's it should've been disclosed."

"Except . . ." Merrill says, "there wasn't a deal to disclose. He had no deal in place at the time he testified."

Anna nods. "Dirty bastards. Prosecutors will do that a lot. We're not going to make a deal with you—wink, wink—but if you testify we'll do what we can for you after the trial. If there's no deal, there's nothing to disclose to the defense, nothing for the jury to hear."

"So he really had a deal," I say, "it just wasn't official, wasn't in writing?"

"Exactly. It wasn't like Justice had anything to lose anyway, but he knew he had a sweet unofficial deal when he stepped into that witness box."

"Think about the charges he was looking at," Merrill says, "yet he out on bail when all this shit with Angel and Qwon happened."

"Convenient coincidence," I say.

"Did he just kill Angel and set Qwon up for it to give himself leverage in his own case?" Anna says.

"Well now," Merrill says. "That's an interesting question, 'cause guess what happen soon as ol' Justice became a witness for the prosecution?"

"Let's see . . ." she says, "his other charges all went away?"

"Exactly. *Poof.* Like magic they vanished."

"So he traded an attempted murder charge for perverting the course of justice, accomplice after the fact," I say.

He nods.

Anna says, "Became a star witness and did six months instead of twenty years. They were probably willing to let him walk, but thought it'd look good to the jury that he was actually going to do a little time."

"All these years later," I say, "and people still mention that. 'Why would he confess to something and serve time for it if he wasn't telling the truth?'"

"I'm sure he was happy to do six months," she says. "Compared to what he *was* looking at."

No one says anything, as we all think about Justice and his role in the case and continuing to eat our breakfast.

"It was a match made in Legal System Hell," Anna says. "He needed to weasel his way out of the pending charges hanging over him and they needed a witness in order to build a case without any physical evidence or even a body."

"It all fits with what you figured out last night," I say.

"What was that?" Merrill asks.

She tells him about Justice's evolving statement and the way he and the cops formed it to fit the cell-phone tower evidence and not the other way around.

"Fits like a mofo," he says.

"Piece by piece," Anna says, "we're taking apart the state's case piece by piece. Soon there'll be nothing left."

Merrill nods. "Qwon's confession still bothers me—and just 'cause Justice lied about some things don't mean he lied about everything. Maybe Qwon was involved. Maybe he helped him kill her and get rid of the body. It's lookin' less and less likely, but . . ."

"Maybe," Anna says, "but I really think Qwon is innocent."

"So . . . y'all ready for my big news?" Merrill says.

"Thought that *was* your big news," Anna says.

"Nah, I was just gettin' to it, working my way up to it. That there was just a little appetizer."

When he doesn't add anything else she says, "Well? Tell us."

"I tracked down Justice's little lying ass," he says.

"You found him?" Anna says. "Where?"

"Just down the road a little ways."

"Well," I say, "let's finish our breakfast and go have a little chat with him."

Chapter Thirty-four

Justice Witney has changed his name to Justin Winslow as part of his attempt at hiding from the world. He lives and works on St. George Island as a condo and beach cottage rental agent.

He's married to a Franklin County school teacher and has two children—a ten-year-old boy and an eight-year-old girl.

We take Highway 71 to Port St. Joe and pick up 98. In Eastpoint we take the four-mile-long St. George Island Bridge, crossing Apalachicola Bay.

St. George Island is a twenty-eight-mile-long and one-mile-wide barrier island, adjacent to Cape St. George in the Apalachicloa Bay. It's a tranquil, if expensive, vacation destination that attracts wealthy families wanting to avoid the madness of Panama City Beach. The eastern end of the island—about nine miles or so—is dedicated to a state park with camping, hiking, and fishing facilities. The peaceful, picturesque island is all sand dunes, sea oats, and pine trees.

Settled early on by Creek Indians who eventually died out due to disease, the island's first Europeans began arriving and fighting for control in the 18th Century. In the 20th Century the island's pine forest was used to harvest turpentine, and during World War

II, St. George was used as a practice range for B-24 bombers.

Justin has a small, single unit in a wooden office building in the business district. We wait until his young office assistant leaves before going in.

It's too early for lunch, so my guess is she's running errands—perhaps to the bank or post office or to check on properties—so I'm not sure how much uninterrupted time we have.

As it turns out, as much as we want. When we walk in, Merrill flips the sign to Closed and locks the door.

"Can I help you?" Justin says, standing from his desk and walking out into the reception area.

Justin Winslow is nothing like Justice Witney. Nothing in his demeanor or dialect remotely resembles the little thug showman from the interviews I'd listened to.

"You sure can," Merrill says. "We need to speak to Justice Witney."

He hesitates a moment, swallowing hard. "There must be some mistake. There's no one here by that name. I'm afraid I need to ask you to unlock my door and leave or I'll have to call the police."

"Justice," I say. "We know who you are and you know we know, so let's not waste a lot of time while you pretend that you're Justin Winslow."

"What do you want?"

"Information," I say. "That's all."

"Well, and maybe a condo for a weekend," Merrill says with a big smile on his face. "It's off sea-son, right? Shouldn't be a problem for you to hook us up."

"Come into my office and let's see if I can't help you both out," he says, turning to walk back into his office.

That was too quick and easy.

"Hold up," I say.

He doesn't stop.

I run over and grab him from behind and pull him away from his desk.

"Whatcha got back there, Justin?" I ask. "Where is it?"

Merrill steps over and pulls him down into one of the two seats in front of his desk. I step behind it and start opening the drawers. There in the middle right side drawer is a Smith .38.

I pull it out and hold it up.

"You can take the thug out of the hood and even change his name," Merrill says, "but . . . can't take the hood out of the thug."

"What were you planning to do with this?" I ask.

"Nothing," he says. "I swear. I just wanted to be able to get to it if I needed to. Think of it from my position."

"Your position is felon," I say. "No way this is legal."

"You barge in my office and lock my door," he continues, ignoring me. "You threaten me and—"

"Nobody's threatened you," I say.

"My bad," Merrill says. "Meant to. Let me correct that oversight right now. Look at me."

Justice looks up at Merrill standing behind him.

"Nobody in this world gonna care what we do to a murderin' drug dealer rat who's let an innocent man sit in prison for almost twenty years. But truth is, nobody'll ever know. Promise you that. It'll be just like that little girl you killed. Your remains will never be found and I won't need a crematorium to destroy them, either. Shit'll be much messier than that. Just like your death. Wet work all the way. So do whatever the fuck you have to do to quit this little bullshit play actin' you doin', and let us talk to Justice. And if Justin ever wants to see his little school teacher wife and kids again, Justice better tell us the goddamn truth and nothin' but the first fuckin' time we ask."

Justice is nodding before he even finishes.

Merrill looks at me. "How was that?"

I nod. "Good. Real good. But let me try one too. Justice, look at me."

He slowly looks away from Merrill, though it's obvious he doesn't want to, and looks at me.

"My associate meant what he said," I say. "Every word of it. But here's a far less violent but no less life-destroying threat for you. We know who you are. We know where you are. Right now we're the only ones who do. Answer our questions honestly and convincingly and it might just stay that way. I'm guessing your clients and business associates don't know who you are and I seriously doubt if your wife and children do."

His response indicates he fears exposure, humiliation, the loss of his reputation and the possible loss of his family even more than physical pain or death.

"That not the kind of shit you put in your chamber of commerce profile or your wedding vows, is it?" Merrill says.

"Thing is," I say. "We're the good guys."

"Fuckin' fightin' on the side of truth and justice," Merrill says.

"We're not here to blow your life up or take you off the board," I say. "We're here for the truth. No agenda other than that. We have some of the pieces. Know some things—like your arrest. Looking for others. Will you answer our questions honestly?"

"Yes, sir. I will. I swear I will."

I ask the first question as a test. "Why'd you cooperate with the cops and prosecutors in Qwon's case?"

"They said I could reduce the charges I was lookin' at by helping them."

"What charges?"

"I got popped a couple of months before for a disagreement I had with a supplier. Bitch said I tried to kill him. They clipped us both for drugs but threw attempted murder on mine. Said they were looking at a classmate of mine. Told me all I had to do was help them put away an innocent rapist and killer and I'd only do a fraction of what I was looking at. I liked Angel. Thought she was a bad bitch. Was glad to help put her killer away—even if at one time I liked him, too. I swear that's the truth."

"Swear it on the lives of your wife and children," Merrill says, "'cause that's what you doin'."

"I swear it on their lives, that's the truth," he says.

I nod.

Merrill moves out from behind Justice and sits in the seat beside him.

I'm about to ask my next question when a Franklin County sheriff's deputy knocks on the door. His gun is out and he actually taps the glass with it.

I pull out my badge and hold it up as I walk toward the door.

Reaching the door, I unlock it and hand him my badge.

"Why is this door locked?" he asks. "Who's in here?

"We just wanted to talk to Mr. Wit—Winslow without being disturbed. I'm John Jordan. I'm with the Gulf County Sheriff's department. With me is Merrill Monroe. He's a licensed investigator. We both have weapons and permits."

"Step out here, Mr. Winslow, Mr. Monroe."

They do.

Merrill is holding up his license and concealed carry permit.

"Everything okay, Mr. Winslow? Your secretary was worried about you."

"I'm fine."

"You sure? You don't seem it."

"I am."

"Mr. Jordan, are you on duty? Does our department know you're here?"

"I'm off duty."

"Okay. I don't know what's going on here, but here's what we're gonna do. I'm gonna call your sheriff and confirm everything but I'm also gonna ask you to leave. This isn't the way to do things—coming in armed and locking the door."

I nod. Now is not the time to reveal who Justin Winslow really is and this deputy is not the person to reveal it to.

"Sorry for how this looks," I say. "We'll be happy to go. There's no need to call my sheriff. Like I've said I'm off duty."

"There a reason you don't want me callin' the Gulf County Sheriff?"

I shake my head. "No," I lie. "Not at all."

Chapter Thirty-five

"What the hell were you thinkin', John?" Reggie says.

We're in her office. Her door is closed.

Reggie Summers, a true country girl, grew up in Wewa and after working security jobs in Central Florida and being Wewa's chief of police for a short time, was appointed by the governor to finish out the term of Gulf County Sheriff when the previous sheriff was killed.

She's not only a great sheriff but a good person and friend. She's the main reason I took this job and have enjoyed it so much.

As soon as she spoke to the Franklin County Deputy she called me and told me to come to her office as fast as humanly possible.

"You can't go into another county and investigate without coordinating it with them. Was it about Daniel? Do you have a new lead? Why didn't you tell me, let me call the Franklin County Sheriff?"

Even seated behind her desk, you can tell Reggie is thick and solid, strong and calm. Tough yet feminine, she's an attractive forty-something who rarely wears makeup or her hair in anything but a ponytail.

I shake my head and frown. "Wasn't about Daniel."

"Then what? Please tell me it's a case Merrill's workin' and you just happened to be along for the ride."

"It's a case he's workin'," I say. "But I'm workin' it too."

"Unofficially? Privately? Why? And why didn't you tell me?"

Her green eyes are even more intense than usual, narrowed and focused.

"Didn't want to get you involved," I say.

"Well, I'm involved now. Is it because it's in Franklin County? Somethin' you stumbled on while looking for Daniel? Does it involve corrupt cops? Help me understand why you wouldn't tell me."

"It's actually a case from Bay County," I say. "Just led us to Franklin—one of the suspects lives there now."

"Bay County? Why the secrecy? Why are you working on a Bay County case?"

"It's a Bay County case . . . that's closed. The man serving time for the crime—eighteen years so far—is an inmate at Gulf. His aunt is a very old friend of mine. Asked me to look into it. I knew I couldn't officially, knew what Bay County's response would be, knew what your response would be."

"You're damn right you did."

"So Merrill and Anna and I have been helping the aunt and stepsister and others look into it."

"Into a closed case in another county?"

I nod.

"What? Two jobs, a wife, two kids, an invalid, and searching for Daniel aren't enough for you?"

"I owed the aunt," I say. "And I think he's truly innocent. I was hoping to be able to prove it. Then I was going to bring it to you."

She shakes her head and lets out a long sigh. "What's the case?"

I tell her.

"What've you got so far?"

I take her through it.

"Fuck," she says. "*Fuck.*"

"I know. I'm sorry."

"Thing is, John, you're not just the best investigator in this department," she says. "You're the best I've ever seen. By a long shot. But . . . it's like basketball. You like basketball, don't you?"

"I used to."

"If you're the greatest player in world—who is that right now? Lebron?"

I nod.

"If you're Lebron and you have all this talent and skill and this amazing instrument, but you don't play with and for your team, you lose. It's not one on one. It's not. You're part of a department now. You can't just do what you want. There's a process, a chain of command, a way of playin' ball."

"I know."

"Thing is . . . I knew this day was coming," she says. "I knew there'd be a day you'd want to cowboy off and do something on your own. You're too good and you've done too many private, unofficial investigations on your own over the years. I knew all that and I still took you on. And up until now you've been great—really and truly respectful and honoring of my position and authority. But this . . . and it doesn't matter that Bay County may have gotten it wrong. Do you know how many innocent people are sitting in prisons all over the world right now because somebody got it wrong? You gonna investigate all those? As a Gulf County investigator? Maybe you need to be private like Merrill. Hell, maybe y'all need to work together to save the world. You'll have some time to think about it . . . because you've left me no other choice but to suspend you. And damn you for doin' that, 'cause you're not just my best investigator, you're my friend, and you've put me in a hell of a bad position."

"I'm truly sorry," I say. "I certainly didn't want to, and was trying not to."

"One week suspension without pay," she says. "And this is how I want you to spend it—finish this damn case, 'cause I know you're not about to stop workin' on it now. But also spend it deciding if you want to be on this team or if you just want to play one on one. One on one is fun and easier and a better fit for certain types of personalities, but you can get a lot more done with a team. A lot more. You have more resources, more help, more everything. I don't want to lose you. I hope you'll decide to stay. I really do. But only if you intend to play team ball and listen to your coach, which, in this metaphor I'm beating to death, is me. Leave your gun and your badge and don't use a single Gulf County Sheriff's department resource while you're on suspension. Don't even say the name. Understand? And while you do that, the adults will continue keeping this place going, taking care of the citizens of this fine county and investigating the whereabouts of Daniel and looking out for each other. Bring me an answer in a week. Make sure you're absolutely sure about it when you do."

Chapter Thirty-six

"I'm sorry," I say to Anna.

I have just told her what happened with Justice and Reggie and about getting suspended.

We are sitting on an old church pew we sawed down to fit in our mud room, talking quietly so we don't disturb Taylor or Sam, who are napping.

"For what?"

"Putting our family at risk," I say. "I could've gotten fired. Still could. What if I had quit my job at the prison and then gotten suspended from the sheriff's department?"

"You didn't," she says. "You wouldn't. You won't. You have nothing to apologize for. For what? Trying to do something good for Ida? Trying to do right by an innocent man—a boy who was unjustly thrown into prison nearly twenty years ago? I'm all in on this too. Right beside you. Every step of the way. Don't apologize and don't stop. Finish this. What do you need?"

I think about it for a moment.

"You're free," she says. "You can do whatever you need to finish the investigation without worrying about any blowback on Reggie."

She's right. I feel a lifting, a lightness—a freedom I haven't felt in a while.

"What will you do with all this newfound freedom?" she asks.

"Start over," I say, nodding slowly. "Go over everything again as if for the first time."

"Whatta you need?"

"The case notes, a computer, and a quiet room."

"We've got all three," she says, smiling at me in the way only she can.

"Thank you."

"Just get in there and use this time and freedom like the gift it is. And take a nap while you're at it."

On the rug on my library floor, the computer on one side, the case notes spread out on the other, I begin by doing a short breathing meditation, attempting to get back to beginner's mind, to, as Rumi says, washing myself of myself, like melting snow.

Start from the beginning. Re-examine everything. Question every assumption.

Who's lying? Who's telling the truth? Forget everything but the actual evidence. What's true? Is anything Justice said true? Anything at all? Is Qwon lying? Was he involved? Did he do it? Was Angel really killed and cremated? Is she even dead? What if she's not? Where is she? Why would she fake her own death?

I begin to read the case file, the notes, the witness statements, the interview transcripts.

The truth is in here. Perceive it. The answers are in here. Listen.

Before long I'm lying on the floor, the papers I was reading on my chest, my heavy eyes closing, my tired body and drowsy mind giving in, letting go, succumbing . . .

When I wake later, I resume my reading, only this time with a much sharper mind, a much more open soul.

Eventually, I put down the papers and just think about the case—about everything I've learned, heard, read.

In a similar fashion to mindful mediation, I let the facts of the case float through my mind, trying not to stop the flow of any, just allowing them to come and go, come and go. I do this for a while, until two of them refuse to float on by, but instead cling—the disposal of Angel's body and her car. Specifically the mileage log she kept, the miles the car traveled after her death.

If I'm truly questioning everything, in a case without a body, I have to question whether Angel is even dead—something I've been doing this entire time, and do again now. As in the times when I've done it before, it leads me nowhere. There is no evidence that she's still alive. None at all.

If Angel is really dead, the second assumption I have to question is whether her remains were really cremated. Justice Witney has lied about so much— why not that? But if Angel's body wasn't cremated, where is it? Why hasn't it been found by now?

And that's when it hits me. What if it has?

How would her body have been found and we not know about it?

Simple. If it hasn't been identified, or if it has been wrongly identified.

And that's where Angel's mileage log and the miles on her car after she disappeared come in.

We had assumed that someone continued to use her car for the month or so between when she went missing and when it was discovered. But what if the car had been used just once for a longer trip instead of every day for shorter ones?

As I find the case notes about Angel's car, I call Kathryn.

"What was Angel wearing the night she went missing?" I ask.

She tells me then asks why.

"Was she wearing any jewelry?"

"A necklace that belonged to her grand-mother—she never took it off—big hoop earrings and a ring with her birthstone in it. A moonstone. Why? Have you found her?"

"Do you know if she had any distinguishing marks on her body?" I ask. "I could ask her parents or Qwon, but if you know, it'd be—"

"She had a scar on the top of her left foot. It was from childhood. Can't remember what happened. Just stands out because she wouldn't wear sandals or flip-flops because she thought it was ugly. She had a birthmark that looked sort of like a shooting star on her right shoulder blade. She may have had others, that's just what stands out at the moment. Did you find her or something?"

"Just wanted the information in case I do."

"You think Justice lied about cremating her?" she asks.

"I think he may have lied about everything," I say. "By the way, we found him."

"What? You did?"

"Talked to him for a little while but got interrupted. We're keeping an eye on him and will talk to him again very soon."

"What'd he say?"

"We'll get together soon and I'll let you know everything I have," I say. "Let me finish running down what I'm working on right now. I'll have Anna call you about coming over for dinner soon."

"Okay. Thanks. And thank you, John, for all you're doing. I can't tell you how much it means."

When I end the call, I look at the notes about Angel's car and open the laptop.

According to the notes Angel's car had been driven nearly six hundred miles after she went missing.

I bring up a map of Florida on the laptop and make a circle three hundred miles in every direction outward from the center of Panama City.

If someone drove her car with her body in it and left her body somewhere and drove back, it couldn't have been more than three hundred miles one way.

Since Panama City is located on the Gulf of Mexico, there are only three directions a car can drive away from it—north, east, and west.

I locate the cities around three hundred miles away in those directions—Biloxi, Mississippi to the west, Atlanta, Georgia to the north, and Jacksonville, Florida to the east—and start calling every jurisdiction from those cities back toward Panama City asking about unidentified late teen female victims with Angel's identifiers.

I start with my second home, Atlanta, and do one of the very things Reggie ordered me not to do—identify myself as a Gulf County sheriff's investigator.

After Atlanta, I call Biloxi, and then Jacksonville, figuring the outer limits of the six hundred mile round trip would be the safest, best place to begin.

Each call takes a while, and all I get is an assurance that somebody will look into it and call me back. I make sure to give them my cellphone and not the office number, hoping this will never get back to Reggie or the department.

Chapter Thirty-seven

Anna and I are eating a late lunch together at the Corner Café, about to discuss possible wedding dates when the calls come.

The first is from Atlanta—swing and a miss. The second from Biloxi is much the same—strike two. But Jacksonville is a solid hit—and may turn into a home run.

The Jacksonville Sheriff's department investigator who calls me back, Robert Van Pelt, is a thoughtful, soft-spoken older man.

"I've been waiting for this call for eighteen years," he says. "And you're not going to believe this . . . but today is my last day on the job. You've given me the best retirement present anyone could."

"You're giving me a gift too," I say.

Anna mouths *Is it her?*

I nod.

She pats my hand and mouths *You're a genius.*

I smile at her.

"I've worried about that poor girl and her family for all these years," Van Pelt is saying. "Can't believe I finally . . . and on my last day with the force."

He sounds like he's talking to himself so I just listen.

"Knew she didn't belong where she was found," he says. "Clean girl like that."

"Where was she found?"

"Old rundown hotel used mostly for prostitution," he says. "We were called out to a lot of deaths, but only one to a girl who looked like this one—no sign of the toll that kind of life takes on them, no premature aging, no drug marks, no old wounds and excessive scars, had all her own teeth. This place was the worst of the worst—could rent a room by the week or the hour. Full of runaways, sex slaves, pimps and prostitutes, junkies, winos. This child didn't belong there. No one does, but you know what I mean."

"Yes, sir, I do."

"What's her name?" he asks.

"The scars and birthmarks match?" I ask.

"Yes they do," he says. "And the necklace and hoop earrings. The moonstone ring was long gone and she'd been stripped naked, but everything else fits. We'll have to get DNA or dental to be certain, but it's her."

"Her name was Angel Diaz," I say.

"Angel Diaz," he repeats in an airy, pensive voice. "And she's from Panama City? I always wondered where she came from."

"Yes, sir. She was."

"Why didn't y'all put her information out?" he asks. "Or check the databases. I input everything and I've been checking at least once a year all these years."

"Witness told the investigators the body had been cremated and they thought they had the guy who did it. Far as they were concerned, case was closed."

"Does this mean they got the wrong guy?"

"It's looking like it," I say.

"Do you know who did it or even exactly what happened to her?"

"No, sir. Not yet. But I'm going to and I'll let you know when I know, if you want me to."

"I'd really appreciate that," he says. "I really would."

"Seeing the autopsy results will really help us in figuring out what happened to her and who did it," I say. "Could you email them to me?"

"No, but I could fax 'em."

I pay Mitchell Johnson, the proprietor of the Corner Café for our lunch, then Anna and I cross Main Street to the bank that will always be Wewa State Bank to me, but is now actually owned by Centennial, to get the fax being sent by Robert Van Pelt.

I have him fax it to our bank not only because of how close it is but because I didn't want to take the chance of anyone at the substation telling Reggie about it.

We retrieve the fax from a very disturbed looking teller and walk over to Lake Alice Park and sit on one of the wooden benches down by the water to read it.

Down by the water's edge, ducks waddle in a straight line, each launching into the water when they reach it, smoothly gliding toward the far corner.

I glance over the autopsy report while telling Anna what Van Pelt said.

"I can't believe he's retiring today," she says.

After a quick perusal of the report I hand it to her.

"Just tell me," she says, though she looks down at it.

"Blunt force trauma to the right side of her head, but she died by strangulation."

"So she was probably stunned or even incapacitated, then while she was dazed or even unconscious she was strangled," she says.

I nod. "No real defensive wounds, so . . . she probably was knocked out by the blow to the head."

"Was she raped?" she asks.

"Looks like it. Signs of vaginal sexual assault."

She shakes her head, frowns, and lets out a long, sad sigh. "Let's hope she was unconscious during that too."

"Appears she may have been," I say. "Some indication it could have been post mortem."

"Oh my God," she says, her face contorting into a combination of revulsion and pain. "What kind of sick little sexual deviant are we looking for? Were they able to get DNA?"

I shake my head. "No semen found. They *did* find traces of lubricant and spermicide like a condom was used."

"Calculating fucker had the presence of mind to put on a condom after killing her but before raping her corpse?"

I shake my head. "What it looks like."

Neither of us says anything for a few moments after that, just sit in silence in the face of such sickness and depravity, in the realization of the brutality Angel was subjected to.

"No alcohol in her system," she says. "Manner of death, homicide."

"Lividity shows what you'd expect if my theory is correct," I say. "She was killed, then laid face down—most likely in the trunk of her car—long enough for the lividity to get fixed, then she was laid on her back on the hotel bed."

"I'd say it's far more than a theory now," she says. "What's next?"

"Have to go public with everything," I say. "Except the sexual assault. Have to involve Reggie and notify the Bay County sheriff's department. Before that we need to tell Angel's family—again, except for the sexual assault. DNA tests or dental records will have to confirm the identity but Van Pelt says he's certain it's her."

"At a minimum Qwon will be granted a new trial," she says, "but I bet he'll be released and not re-tried."

I nod. That's something, but it's not the same as figuring out who actually did it.

"Justice lied about cremating the body," she says. "What else did he lie about?"

"Maybe everything."

"He and the cops and the prosecutors have lots of "splainin' to do," she says.

Chapter Thirty-eight

What happens next happens fast.

Anna and I walk back home.

I call Reggie and explain to her what we have.

"Son of a bitch, John," she says. "I mean *fuck*."

"I know."

"Good work, though," she says. "I mean it. That's what matters most. The truth. Justice. Protecting the innocent. Finding the guilty—speaking of, do you know who actually killed her?"

"Not yet."

"Okay. I'll deal with Bay County. I'm sure they'll have questions. I'll need you to meet with them. Will let you know."

"Thanks."

"No, thank you. I mean it. Outstanding work. The little jurisdictional headaches and the embarrassment to Bay County is nothing compared to finding her body and bringing her home to her family. Nothing. I'll be in touch."

I call Merrill next and tell him.

"How long 'fore this all blow up in the media?" he asks.

"A few days at most."

"So we need to keep watchin' Justice 'til then."

"Yeah. You need help?"

"Got a couple of guys helping me," he says. "He ain't changed his routine or done anything suspicious."

"When we meet with Bay County I'll let them know where he is. I'm sure they'll want to talk to him."

"'Cause that shit went so well last time."

I laugh.

"You gonna be cool with just turnin' this back over to them?"

"Don't have a choice," I say. "Unless . . ."

"'Less what?"

"We turn up something else or figure something else out before they reopen the investigation."

"I'a see what I can do."

I call Ida next.

"Thank you, boy," she says. "You can't know what that means to me. And to her poor parents. Do they know yet?"

"I'm about to go tell them now."

"Bless you, boy. Bless you for what you've done. I'll see you in a few days. Gonna hug your neck so hard, squeeze the breath out of you."

After kissing Anna and Taylor goodbye, I head to Panama City to talk to Buck and Kay Diaz.

On the way I call Kathryn.

When I tell her she bursts into tears and for several miles I just listen as she cries and is unable to speak.

"Sorry," she says, eventually.

"Don't be."

"I'm just . . . I've waited so long for this. Qwon has been inside for eighteen years. No one would help. No one would even take us seriously. I'm just . . . overwhelmed. Does he know yet? Does Ida?"

"Ida does. He doesn't. I'll tell him later this afternoon when I go to the prison. Right now I'm on the way to tell Angel's parents."

"If I can get him on the phone, would you mind if I tell him?" she says.

"Not at all. I had planned to have him come to my office and I was going to call you so you could. But go ahead and tell him if you can. If not, let me know and I'll have him call you this evening when I get there."

"Thank you, John. Thank you for everything."

Chapter Thirty-nine

I meet with Buck and Kay Diaz in their small home on Jenks Avenue not far from downtown—the same house they had raised Angel in.

Like the childless parents who dwell inside it, the house is shrouded in sadness, its muted colors and general state of neglect signs of grief, evidence of mourning.

Buck meets me at the door and welcomes me in.

Kay serves us coffee in the small living room where a plethora of framed photos of Angel are displayed.

The photographs show an only child growing up in nothing less than complete and utter adoration. Sadly, even the most recent of the pictures are aged and dated and beginning to fade, the image they hold that of a teenager on the verge of adulthood who will never grow any older, who will never be photographed again, who will never be pictured graduating or with friends or her spouse on their wedding day or her children on Christmas morning or grandchildren at an Easter egg hunt.

Like the girl in the photographs, the house itself seems trapped in time, and I wondered if anything has been changed since the night Angel never came home.

Or did she? Amber and Kathryn saw her car here on their way home that night. What does that mean—especially in the light of what we know now? Did something happen here? Is this where she was killed? Had one or both of her parents done it and covered it up?

Buck sits in an old, worn recliner, his wife on the couch. Unlike the first time I met with them, there seems to be distance, even coldness between them.

In the corner, which holds what can only be described as a shrine to Angel—with pictures, candles, and other mementos—sits a chair that must have been hers, given the way they both directed me away from it.

"Is this another interview," Buck says, "or do you have news?"

"Just let him say what he wants to," Kay says.

"I have news," I say. "It may be of some comfort to you but it will also be difficult to hear. You need to take a moment to prepare yourself to hear it."

In unison, they set their coffee cups down, sit back in their seats, and take in a deep breath.

Across from them in a small, uncomfortable chair, I too put my coffee cup down.

"We're waiting for positive scientific confirmation," I say, "but we believe we've found what really happened to Angel's body after her death."

Kay breaks down.

"You *believe*?" Buck says. "What does that—"

"I wouldn't be here if we weren't fairly certain," I say. "But we have to wait for confirmation before we can be absolutely certain. I just didn't want you to hear it another way."

Buck's dark hair seems thinner and grayer now, as if grief is actually leeching life out of him, and after what I've just said, his dark, orangish complexion has drained to a clammy pasty pale.

I look over at Kay. Her pale skin is even paler, if possible, and her green eyes, wet with tears, have taken on the hue of the Gulf after a storm.

Instead of late fifties and mid sixties, both Kay and Buck appear to be in their late seventies.

"What happened to her?" Kay asks.

I tell them what we know.

"So she—her body wasn't cremated?" Buck says.

Ironically it had been eventually, following Jacksonville's inability to identify her and in the absence of any family claiming her.

"Not by Justice," I say. "Not like he said."

"That lying piece of shit," Buck says. "He—his lies kept us from our little girl's remains all these years. I'm gonna kill that nigger bastard. I swear to Christ I am."

"Shut up, Buck," Kay says. "You're gonna do no such thing."

He jerks his head over at her and their eyes lock. Neither of them say anything, but what passes between them is palpable.

Eventually Kay looks back at me. "Do you know who killed my baby girl?"

I shake my head. "Not yet. But we're certainly getting closer and this is a big step in that direction. Looks even more like Qwon had nothing to do with it now."

She nods slowly, wipes tears from her cheeks and the corners of her eyes.

"I'm so sorry," I say. "I'm sorry this happened to Angel. I'm sorry you've had to live with all the unknowns and unanswered questions all these years. I'm sorry you had to hear this today."

"How did she die?" Buck asks.

I hesitate a moment.

"Please," Kay says.

"She was strangled," I say. "But it looks like she was hit on the head first. She was probably unconscious after that so didn't feel any . . . thing . . . or know what was happening."

"*Probably*?" Buck says. "*Probably*?"

"Buck, stop," Kay says.

"I'm sorry," I say.

"You're sorry," Buck says. "Everybody's sorry. So damn sorry. When can we get her remains? When can we bury our baby?"

I swallow hard and wish I was somewhere else, anywhere else in the world, at this moment.

"I'm sorry," I say again, "but after six months . . . the city of Jacksonville . . . cremated her remains and . . . scattered her ashes in the Atlantic Ocean."

Kay begins to sob. Buck jumps up and starts breaking things, beginning with his own hand, but continuing with the TV, a bookshelf, and several glasses and dishes in the kitchen. What he doesn't break, or even come close to, however, even as out of control as he seems, is any of the pictures or mementos of Angel.

While Buck is wreaking havoc in his own house, Kay never looks up, never does anything but wail into her hands—the hands that had held and hugged and cleaned and comforted and fed her little girl. The little girl who is gone now. Utterly and completely and irrevocably gone. Ashes in the Atlantic. Out to sea. Never to return, not at any time, not with any tide.

Chapter Forty

The next day Merrill, Anna, Kathryn, and I meet with an investigator with the Bay County Sheriff's department.

We give him everything we have. Everything. Hold back nothing. And in doing so I turn the case over to him, return it to the agency that investigated it the first time, giving them an opportunity at a certain kind of redemption.

The day after that Angel's identity is confirmed by dental records.

Two days later the Bay County Sheriff and the state's attorney hold a joint press conference.

Neither man was in the position he now holds when Angel's investigation and Qwon's trial took place, which makes what they do now all the more palatable for them. So does having scapegoats.

Both men apologize on behalf of their agencies and call out those to blame by name—a disgraced investigator who had long since been fired and the former state's attorney who had been a bitter political rival of the current one.

"We are officially reopening the Angel Diaz murder case," the sheriff says.

"And," the state's attorney adds, "dismissing the charges against and releasing Acqwon Lewis. I've filed a motion with the court and Mr. Lewis's release is imminent. There's also going to be an investigation into those involved in the case—specifically the investigator and prosecutor. We will get to the bottom of how such a grievous miscarriage of justice took place."

The sheriff then finds the camera and looks directly into it. "And to the person or persons responsible for Angel Diaz's death, know this—you may have gotten away with it until now, but your days are numbered. There's a net and it's closing in on you. Soon you will be in custody. You *will* pay for what you did. We will not rest until you are behind bars for good."

As I'm watching the press conference in my office at the prison, my phone rings.

"Nice work on finding the body," Randa says. "Using the mileage on the car like that . . . pretty impressive."

I don't say anything.

We have searched our home and vehicles for bugs and haven't found any, so I assume she's getting the information she has by hacking into computers and phones, but she consistently seems to know more than what she would learn just by hacking our devices.

"Couldn't help but notice nobody mentioned your name at the press conference," she says.

"Didn't mention Anna or Merrill or Kathryn or you either," I say. "No one thought they would."

"Fine by me if they never mention my name," she says.

"Feel the same way."

"How'd you find Justice and the information about his arrest?" she asks.

"I didn't. Merrill did."

"Exactly," she says. "Without that you don't get to the car and the body, so . . . I'm afraid I'm gonna have to call off our little bet. You're not doing all the work by yourself like I am. You've got a team."

"You're welcome to join it," I say. "Let's meet up and discuss it."

"Always tryin' to get with me," she says. "Does Anna know about this?"

"Yeah, she's all for it."

She laughs. "I bet she is."

I don't respond.

"How's your ego feeling, John?"

"Why do you ask, Randa?"

"Would you be able to handle it if I beat you twice in a row and once and for all?"

"Thought you just called off our little bet?" I say.

"We both know you never really agreed to that. That was just me having a bit of fun. You know . . . got to find it where you can. Anyway, so here's the deal, if I solve the case right now you never look for me or Daniel again."

"You can solve it right now?" I ask.

"Told you I'm a lot better at this than you."

"Does Daniel want to stay with you?" I ask.

"Would I be able to keep him here if he didn't?"

"At this point I believe you can do about any-thing."

"That's so sweet, John. Really is. Means a lot coming from someone like you."

"If and only if Daniel himself tells me he wants to be with you—and convinces me that he really means it—and you really and truly solve the case . . . you have a deal."

"I have your word?" she says.

"You have my word."

"Then I'll tell you what I'm going to do," she says. "I'll go ahead and solve the case for you now—and let you go ahead and save Qwon and make the arrest and all. Then a little later, after you've done all that, I'll let Daniel give you a call and y'all can have a little chat."

"Does Qwon need saving?" I ask.

"Yeah, I'm afraid so. So here it is. The cops were right about the ex. They just arrested the wrong one. It wasn't Angel's ex. It was Qwon's. Zelda Sager was there that night. She may have even made out with Qwon and tried to rekindle things with him, though from what I hear he was so messed up . . . he probably didn't know who he was making out with or what he was doing."

I recall Qwon's dream or fragments of memo-ries that he had made out with an ex-girlfriend that night.

"She killed Angel," she says. "To get Qwon back or because she's just nuts. I don't know. But . . . there you go."

"That's not evidence," I say, "just accusation."

"Maybe, but it's still true."

"Unless you've got more than that," I say, "I wouldn't call it solving the case."

"Well, either I'm right or I'm not, but there's another little piece of the puzzle you should know. Zelda's husband is Troy Payne. And he's a sergeant at your prison, isn't he?"

I jump up.

"John?" she says, as I drop the phone. "John? You there?"

Chapter Forty-one

Jogging down the compound toward Confinement I'm acutely aware of how new I am to this institution.

I can't call Merrill or Anna like I once could at Potter Correctional, and though I've made some friends and earned some respect here at Gulf CI, I'm not sure who I would call even if there was time to do it.

As I near confinement, a young African-American CO I don't recognize falls in beside me, matching my pace, and says, "Everything okay, Chaplain?"

"Need to check on an inmate in Confinement," I say. "You got a minute to help?"

"Sure," he says.

"May involve stopping a sergeant who's abusing him," I say. "That gonna be a problem for you?"

"Who's the sergeant?"

"Payne," I say.

"Hell, nah," he says. "That fuc—He's a . . . No, sir. Won't be a problem."

We're buzzed through the gate of the fence that surrounds the confinement building by the officer in Tower II, then through the door of confinement itself by an officer in the control room.

Through the glass of the officers' station I can see that Payne isn't inside it—just an overweight mid-thirties white guy slumped down in a small office chair.

I run over to it and speak to the officer inside through the document tray.

He rolls in his chair over to where we're standing. Slowly. Apathetically.

"Is Sergeant Payne on duty?" I ask.

He nods.

"Where is he?"

He shrugs. "On one of the wings somewhere, I guess. Really don't know."

"Which cell is Acqwon Lewis in?" I ask.

He slowly lifts a clipboard and looks at it. "B-11"

"Can you buzz us through?"

"Sign in," he says.

As I sign in, he looks at the young officer with me and says, "What can I help you with?"

"I'm here with the chaplain."

"Huh? I can let the chaplain in. I can't just let other random COs in."

"Really?"

"Not without some kind of authorization. Ain't about to lose this cushy job over not following procedure."

I turn to the young officer. "What's your name?"

"Jay Nobles, sir."

"Go get the OIC or the Colonel, Jay, and bring them back down here," I say. "Fast as you can."

"Yes, sir."

The officer in the control room buzzes me onto B block and Jay Nobles out the front door.

I run down toward Qwon's cell.

The hallway is darker and quieter than usual.

As I near it, I see that Qwon's cell door is open.

Inside I find Troy Payne beating a cuffed Qwon with a thick wooden officer's baton.

Qwon is on the floor trying his best to gather himself in a fetal position and protect his head, even though his hands are cuffed behind him.

I enter the cell and yell for Payne to stop.

He turns toward me, a madness in his distant eyes. "'Less you want some too, you need to get from in here."

"I'm not cuffed," I say.

"Won't matter," he says.

And he's right.

He's younger, faster, stronger, and has far more rage than me. I'm no match for him—and wouldn't be even if he didn't have a baton.

As I lunge for the baton, he sidesteps me more quickly than I would have thought him capable, and jams the end of the baton into my abdomen.

When I fall forward and grab at my stomach, trying to get my breath back, he backhands me with it.

I raise my right arm instinctively, defensively, and manage to bock part of the blow, but my arm pays the price.

Arcs of pain fire through my arm, up my shoulder, through my body.

I kick at him, missing the first time but connecting with the second.

He stumbles backwards and trips over Qwon, smacking his head on the stainless steel toilet as he goes down.

He drops the baton and as he scrambles around to get it and get back to his feet, I grab Qwon with my left arm and pull him toward the door.

He begins to push with his legs and kind of half crawl, helping in our progress.

I manage to get Qwon out into the hallway, but as I'm stepping over to shove the cell door closed, Payne comes charging toward me.

That's when I make a serious mistake in calculation.

Instead of lifting my arms to protect myself or trying to tackle him, I attempt to close the cell door.

I don't get it closed in time.

Payne takes advantage of my defenseless position, raising the baton up over his head and bringing it hard down on mine.

And that's it.

Closing time.

The bartender inside my head says *You don't have to go home, but you got to get the hell up outta here.*

And then the lights go out.

And then nothing.

Chapter Forty-two

When I come to, Jay Nobles is looking down at me.

"You okay, Chaplain?"

I nod—but when I do it hurts. "Where is—" I turn to look for Qwon and Troy Payne.

"Everything's okay," he says.

Troy Payne is cuffed and standing twenty feet or so down the hallway, a captain and another CO standing with him, each with an arm on his shoulder.

Qwon is closer, only five feet away, a nurse examining him.

"Help me up," I say.

"Just wait, the nurse hasn't examined you yet."

I start to get up slowly. "I can do it on my own or you can help me."

He helps me to my feet and I hold onto him for a moment to steady myself as my head pounds, my stomach turns, and the hallway spins.

"You okay?" he asks softly so only I can hear.

I nod. "Thanks"

The colonel walks over to me.

"Hey," Payne yells to him. "Why am I cuffed? What's going to happen to—"

"You're going to jail," I say.

"What happened here, Chaplain?" the colonel asks.

I tell him—about the case, about Zelda, about Payne's abuse of Qwon and his motive for it.

"I was told that Inmate Lewis was being released," he says.

I nod, wincing as I do.

"You work for the sheriff's department, right? Were you serious about taking him to jail?"

I nod again, and remind myself it's not a good idea. "I'm sure he'll face a DC investigation and discipline, but we need to interview him in connection with the Angel Diaz case. And I witnessed his assault on Qwon."

He nods. "Okay. He's all yours." He turns to walk away, then turns back. "And . . . nice work, Chaplain. Welcome to GCI. Happy to have you aboard."

When I get home, the deadbolt is on and I can't get in.

I ring the doorbell and send Anna a text, letting her know I'm outside.

When she opens the door, she quickly looks out and all around as I walk in.

"Chris was released today," she says.

"Have you seen or heard from him?"

"No. Is that blood on your head? Are you okay?"

"I'm fine. Qwon was released today too. Zelda's husband wasn't too keen on that and took a baton to my head."

"What?"

I tell her.

"Are you okay? How bad does it hurt?"

"Being home has it feeling better already."

"You can't imagine how happy I am to have you home. Do you have to go back out? Did you interview Payne already?"

I shake my head. "Handed him off to Bay County. They picked up Zelda too."

"Really? You're okay with that?"

I nod. "Played my part in it. Qwon is out, the investigation is reopened."

"But don't you want to be involved still? Don't you want to be the one to solve it, to build the case, make the arrest?"

"Always want to, but . . . I'm fine with my role in this one. We have Chris and a thousand other things to deal with. I helped get Ida's nephew out."

"You didn't just *help*. You're the *reason* he's out. By the way, Ida called. They're having a homecoming party for Qwon tomorrow night. She's coming down from Atlanta for it. They really want us there."

Chapter Forty-three

Somehow Kathryn convinced the owner of the old Fiesta and La Royale Lounge buildings to let her throw Qwon's homecoming party in the courtyard between them.

And it's perfect.

Strings of small white lights strewn all around provide subtle illumination. Soft music from a PA system sets the mood. An open bar on one side. A table of catered finger foods on the opposite side across from it. A small riser stage with a mic and mic stand in back by what was once Bubba's office. Next to it a large framed photograph of Angel is surrounded by flowers and candles. Patio tables in the center. People sitting, milling about, hugging an overwhelmed Qwon.

The crowd consists primarily of Angel and Qwon's school friends—McKenna Roberts, Billy Anderson, Rex Timberson, Derrick Edwards, Paige Askew—many of whom walked through downtown with me and Kathryn last week working on the case. Both Angel and Qwon's parents are present. So is Ida.

There are a few people I don't recognize—at least two of which I'd guess did time with Qwon at some point.

Eric Pulsifer is also present. I wasn't sure he'd show.

Merrill and Za are here.

So is the Bay County Sheriff's investigator in charge of the reopened case.

Anna and I and Merrill and Za are standing near the back, which is actually the front, near the wrought iron gate on the Harrison side, cups in hand, watching.

We are able to be here because Dad and Verna are at our house with Taylor and Sam. And Dad has his .45 in case Chris shows up.

"Thank you for what you did, boy," Ida says, as she hugs me.

"It was a group effort," I say. "Anna and Merrill did as much as I did—probably more. Za helped too."

She thanks and hugs them too.

"Y'all just can't know what this does for a sad old woman's heart."

"We're very happy for that," Merrill says.

She calls Qwon over to us.

"You thanked these good people enough yet, boy?" she asks.

"No, ma'am. It's not possible. Plan to thank them every day of my free life."

"How're your head and ribs?" I ask.

"Sore," he says, "but for some reason they feel a lot better out here than they did inside. How's your head?"

"Was hoping the blow knocked some sense into me, but . . . nothing so far."

"He never let on he had any connection to my case," he says. "That he was with Zelda. I just thought he was a sadistic prick. Sorry, Aunt Ida."

"For what? Sounds like that's exactly what he was."

"Anyway, thanks for saving my life," he says to me.

"Yes, John," Ida says. "Thank you for that too."

"Anybody not here you thought would be?" I ask Qwon.

"You still workin' on the case?" he asks.

"He never stops," Anna says.

"Yeah," he says. "I was surprised not to see Darius and Amber. Katie said they helped you in the investigation. Just figured they'd be here."

Kathryn steps up onto the little riser stage and takes the mic from the stand.

"Hey," she says. "Can you hear me?"

People stop talking and someone turns the music down but not off.

"I wanted to thank you all for coming out to help us celebrate tonight," she says. "This has been a long, long, long time in the making. I'm so glad we get to do it here. For many of us this was the last place we were truly young, free, and happy. I have to say . . . that as happy as I am that Qwon is out here with us where he belongs, I am equally sad that Angel is not."

She glances over at the picture of Angel surrounded by flowers and candles. Everyone follows her gaze. She then looks at Angel's parents.

"It means so much to us that Buck and Kay can be here with us tonight," she says. "They have always believed in Qwon's innocence and their support has been astounding. Their presence and this memorial of Angel are reminders that this isn't over. We celebrate that an innocent man is out of prison, but we won't stop until the guilty one is inside."

The group cheers and whistles at that.

"With that in mind, I want to thank John Jordan for helping free Qwon. He and his wife, Anna, and their friend Merrill Monroe are the reason we're here tonight. I want to also say how happy we are that the case has been reopened and that the investigator in charge of it is also with us tonight. Randy Pinter is going to make sure we get justice for Angel this time."

Randy waves and the small crowd gives him a round of polite but anemic applause.

"Now, without further ado I give you the man of the hour," she says. "Mr. Acqwon Lewis."

Chapter Forty-four

Qwon makes his way to the stage and the two hug for a long moment.

When she hands him the mic and steps away and he turns to face the group, he breaks down and begins to sob.

The small gathering gives him audible love and support.

"We love you, Qwon," Billy, his former classmate yells.

"I . . . love . . ."

Qwon tries to speak a few times, but is unable. Eventually, he composes himself enough to get through it.

"I can't tell y'all how happy I am tonight," he says.

His voice is thick and hoarse and he sniffles a lot.

"I honestly never thought this day would come. And it wouldn't have if it weren't for my amazing sister, Kathryn Lewis. Just like her to thank everyone else, but not mention herself. She's been my biggest supporter and believer. And my folks. Thank you, Dad, Mom. I love y'all. And Buck and Kay. I love and appreciate y'all more than you'll ever know. I'm so, so, so sorry for what happened to our Angel. The only thing that bothered me more than being in prison for something I didn't do was knowing whoever did it was still free. But he's not free for long."

The crowd cheers.

"Mom, Dad," he says, holding up the mic, "want to say anything?"

Henry and Mary Elizabeth step up on the stage.

"We can't tell you how hard this has been on our family," Mary Elizabeth says "or how happy we are tonight or how proud we are of both our children."

"So we won't try," Henry says. "Thank you all for your support, for coming tonight, and please, please help us find the monster who killed Angel. Thank you."

They step off the stage and the four of them, a family again, hug.

The music is turned back up. People begin to talk and move around again, to eat and drink and laugh and eventually even dance.

I turn and look out on Harrison, scanning the area around us—the empty buildings across the street, the vacant sidewalks, the quiet night in the abandoned downtown.

"What is it?" Anna asks.

"Just wondering if Randa is out there somewhere watching us," I say.

"I hope she's in another country," she says. "Except . . . I hope Daniel is not that far away. Do you think she really could be watching us?"

"I think she knows too much not to be keeping tabs on us and the investigation—"

"We want to apologize for our behavior," Kay Diaz says.

I turn around to see her and Buck standing there.

"The way we acted when you were at our house," she continues, "was . . ."

"Understandable," I say. "Don't give it another thought."

Buck nods and extends his hand. I shake it.

Kay hugs me and they move on.

The crowd begins to thin out some, but all the family and close friends stay.

Eventually Darius and Amber arrive, and I wonder if they came together. If so, that's an interesting development. Or is it? Maybe it's not a development at all—at least not a recent one. Maybe they've been secretly together for a while now.

Long after I would have normally left an event like this, we are sitting at one of the patio tables—Anna, Merrill, Za, and me.

"You want to watch everyone for as long as you can, don't you?" Anna says.

I nod. "Especially as they drink."

And people are drinking. No one more than Buck and Kay, but everybody except me and Randy.

Randy Pinter, the Bay County Sheriff's investigator, ambles over toward us.

"Pull up a chair," I say.

He does.

Someone, McKenna I believe, puts on 90s music, turns it up, and the classmates wind up on the dance floor together, dancing to Sugar Ray, Destiny's Child, Christina Aguilera, Cher, Britney Spears, the Goo Goo Dolls, Santana and Rob Thomas, taking turns dancing with Qwon, acting as if this is a class reunion instead of what it is.

"Payne says he was a little tough on Acqwon because he thought he was a killer and he knew his wife had once been involved with him," Pinter says. "Says maybe he got a little carried away, but . . . nothing more than that."

I rub the bump on my head. "A little carried away, huh? What's Zelda say?"

"Haven't located her yet," he says. "She wasn't at their house and hasn't been back. We'll find her."

"I really think you will," I say, nodding toward the entrance and the woman I recognize from pictures on Troy Payne's Facebook page.

There, just inside the wrought iron gate, Zelda Sager stands staring at her former classmates.

"Well, how about that," Pinter says. "Payne says she didn't have anything to do with Angel's death and that the only reason he was so *tough* on Acqwon was because he was jealous. He thinks she still has a thing for him."

I look back at the dancing group. None of them have seen her yet.

Seeing them dance the way they are, seeing Zelda standing watching, it all comes together for me—all the facts and evidence and possibilities coalesce into a narrative of what happened that night and I finally know what happened.

I finally know who killed Angel Diaz.

Chapter Forty-five

Anna looks at me. "You know, don't you?"

I look back at her. "I think I do."

Zelda is actually joined at the entrance by Justice Witney and I see an opportunity beginning to form.

"Oh shit," Pinter says. "Is that who I think it is?"

"It is. You mind if I see if I can't use the energy and emotion here to try to get a confession?"

"Be my guest," he says. "Just let me record it and try to work in a Miranda warning if you can."

"What the fuck?" Billy says. "What're they doin' here?"

"Son of a bitch," Darius says.

The group begins to move toward Zelda and Justice.

Merrill, Pinter, and I jump up and rush toward them.

"Come on in," I say. "Let them in. Listen to what they have to say. And somebody turn off the music. Please."

Justice and Zelda slowly step in. The group stops where they are.

I'm about to ask Merrill to guard the door, but he's already blocking it with his massive frame.

"The police are looking for y'all," McKenna says.

"I had to see you," Zelda says to Qwon. "Can we talk?"

"The fuck are you doin' here?" Billy says to Justice.

Everyone starts to form a circle around the showdown—including Ida and Qwon and Angel's parents.

Pinter, Anna, and Za have their phones out recording.

"Qwon," Justice says. "I'm sorry man. They told me you did it. I . . . I thought you did it. I wouldn't just lie against you like that. The cops said they knew you did it . . . just needed a witness to give testimony. I swear man. I was a punk ass bitch back then and I'm sorry. Sorry for all the wrong I done, but I wouldn't just make shit up about you on something like this if the cops hadn't told me you did it."

"We know who killed Angel," I say. "We know how it happened and who did it."

"This son of a bitch, right?" Billy says.

"Y'all want to have this out, get this over with once and for all?" I say. "Right now?"

"Hell, yeah," Qwon says.

The others follow his lead.

"We can finish this right now," I say. "Here and now. After almost twenty years. All y'all have to do is agree to it."

"We agree," Billy says.

"Agree to this being an official interview," I say. "Agree to waive your Miranda rights, that you don't have to say anything, but if you do . . . it can be used against you. Everybody agree to that?"

They all nod.

"Need to hear everyone say it. Everyone here—even the parents."

Everyone verbally agrees. Anna, Za, and Pinter record them doing it.

And so I dive in.

"It was a wild, wonderful, magic night," I say. "The kind that nothing bad can happen on—or so most of us probably thought. You guys were happy—happy as angst-ridden teenagers get. You were full of life and love and alcohol and drugs and—the group here at the Fiesta was essentially having an orgy on the dance floor."

"It's true, we were," Amber says.

"We really did feel so much . . . love," McKenna says.

"Old feelings got stirred up," I say. "New feelings got stirred up."

"Blame it on the a-a-a-a-a-alcohol," Billy says.

"Qwon's been having a recurring nightmare or fragments of guilt-ridden memories all these years," I say. "He dreams or remembers making out with an old girlfriend. And he did. And that's what got Angel killed."

Several people look at Zelda.

"How?" MeKenna says. "Tell us how."

"Angel was at Kim and Ken's but was bored and decided to walk back up toward Fiesta, which she did," I say. "And that single act, that decision determined her fate. Because when she got close she saw Qwon making out with another girl—and not just any girl. An old girlfriend. And not just any making out, but a passionate, true love kind of making out. But as bad as all that was, what bothered her even more, what disturbed her to her core was who he was making out with. His own sister, Kathryn."

Chapter Forty-six

The reaction everyone gives is what I expect.

Ida, Kay, and Mary Elizabeth gasp.

Several of Kathryn's classmates, including Amber and McKenna, and Paige, shake their heads.

"It all came together for me when I saw y'all dancing and remembered that night," I say.

"No fuckin' way, man," Billy says. "There's just no way."

Qwon looks at Kathryn, the sadness and guilt and betrayal palpable.

"There's a reason why Kathryn dedicated her life to freeing Qwon," I say. "Even went to law school. Never got married or had kids. But in all that time she wasn't really going after anyone else, just trying to free Qwon. Both because she loves him, but also because she's actually guilty of the crime. It's why she had the defense team do polygraphs of all the witnesses—but limited them to questions about Qwon. Ordinarily a test like that would ask 'Did you kill Angel Diaz?' or 'Do you know who did? or 'Did you have anything to do with the death of Angel Diaz?' Questions like that."

Henry and Ida stare at me in shock and confusion. Mary Elizabeth is crying. Buck is growing angrier by the second. Kay is weeping quietly.

"Qwon and Kathryn had dated before their parents ever met," I say. "And Kathryn was still in love with him. Maybe he was still in love with her, too. Maybe in his drug-altered state he kissed her and loved her like he used to. He had gone out to get more alcohol and ecstasy out of his car. Kathryn followed him and asked him to grab her jacket, but he didn't hear her. She stayed out there, said she was getting fresh air, but she was waiting for him. She lied and said she saw Justice walking down Beach Drive—something she's never mentioned before, but Derrick walked down Beach around that time from the park and never saw him. When Qwon came back, high and drunk and touchy feely, he and Kathryn began kissing and making out, maybe even started having sex. They weren't the first or the last to do so out there."

"No," Mary Elizabeth says.

"They wouldn't do that," Henry adds.

"Oh, my God," Qwon says. "We . . . we . . . Oh God."

I think about Qwon's dreams and memories and wonder how little he really remembers. How much is a black hole of alcohol and drugs—including more than just ecstasy and maybe even GHB—and how much is the result of PTSD and repression?

The group of classmates pulls back from Kathryn and Qwon. It's slight, nearly imperceptible, but it happens.

I look over at Ida, trying to gage her reaction. We've been here before.

"No, Son," Henry says. "You wouldn't do that."

"No," Mary Elizabeth says. "Please no."

"I was . . . so out of it," Qwon says. "I . . . she's not my sister."

"She's your stepsister," Henry says.

Darius shakes his head. "I was so in love with you," he says to Kathryn. "While I was inside watching your drink so nobody put anything in it, you were outside fucking your brother in the parking lot like a goddamn dog. All these years I . . . I carried a torch for you. You were the one that got away. What a fuckin' fool."

"Your friends called you *Jungle Fever*," I say to Kathryn. "But it wasn't as general as they thought, was it? It wasn't black guys. You had it bad for one guy in particular—Qwon, who happened to be black."

She won't look at me in the eye.

"What was I?" Darius says, "a fuckin' substitute? A beard? Is that why you wouldn't sleep with me? Because of *him*?"

"Angel walked up and saw them," I say.

"Honey, please tell me he's wrong," Mary Elizabeth says to Kathryn.

Kathryn is crying now, looking down, shaking her head.

Everyone continues to distance themselves from her, even her parents. She's growing more and more isolated.

"Angel saw y'all and Kathryn saw her."

"You did?" Qwon says to her. "*I* never saw her. You really did? Oh God . . . she must have thought . . . the last thing she thought was . . ."

"While Qwon went back in the club—we know he went in alone because Amber said she grabbed him and danced with him, but never mentioned Kathryn because she didn't come back in until later. She chased Angel down to . . . what?"

"Just to explain," Kathryn says, looking up, but not making eye contact. "To say he wasn't really my brother. That we were together before our parents ruined it for us. To tell her it wasn't sick or perverted or anything that she thought and . . . to apologize to her. I was so sorry for what we had done, and that she had seen it."

"What happened?" I ask.

"She wouldn't stop or even slow down," Kathryn says. "Wouldn't . . . She kept saying she was going to tell everyone, that she was going to let everyone know how sick we were. She was upset, like repulsed, and she kept yelling as she ran. I asked her to stop, to stop running, to stop yelling before someone heard her, but she wouldn't. Said she was going to tell our parents and everyone at school. I . . . I didn't mean to kill her . . . I mean . . . I didn't intend to. I was just trying to talk to her, to get her to quit running and yelling and . . . but she wouldn't. I was just trying to get her to let me explain, but she wouldn't."

Mary Elizabeth keeps shaking her head, wiping tears. "This can't be . . ."

Henry can no longer look at Kathryn, but Buck can. He's staring at her with a frightening, fiery intensity.

Kathryn and Qwon's classmates look on in stunned silence, their faces masks of confusion and revulsion.

"Did she make it to her car?" I say.

"She stumbled and tripped as she got close to it—which just made her more hysterical. She was so . . . She just lost it and so did I. I had been drinking and . . . I had so much adrenaline and fear and . . . all just pumping through me. I . . . I grabbed her as she tried to get up. She . . . jerked away. I . . . I grabbed her even harder and shook her—just trying to get her to calm down, but she wouldn't. It only made it worse. She called me a slut and a whore and a . . . said I committed incest and that soon everyone would know it, that mine and Qwon's lives would be ruined. I . . . I just snapped. Just like that. So much rage. I slammed her head against the tire well of her car and . . . just . . . wrapped my hands around her throat."

She makes eye contact for the first time, searching the gathered group for understanding, for any hint of compassion.

"I was so . . ." she begins, then stops. "It was like I was outside of my body, like I was watching someone else do it. I'm so sorry. So sorry. Please forgive me."

"Never," Buck yells and charges her.

I grab him from the front and Pinter gets him from the back.

We pull him away from her and he shrugs us off and walks back over to his wife and hugs her, breaking down and crying with her.

I turn back to her. "Was it premeditated?"

"*No,*" she says. "Absolutely not."

"When did you take the keys from Qwon?"

"I—"

"When you first saw her?" I ask. "When you and Qwon were still . . . being intimate and you had access to his pockets or—"

"No. Absolutely not. I went back for them. I rolled her body under her car. Went back for them. I swear. I . . . I made sure everyone saw me again. Took his keys while we danced. Went back and . . ."

"Put Angel's body in the trunk," I say.

She nods.

"Then hid it. Did you take it home then or just hide it somewhere else?"

"I . . . I hid it then. Later when we were all looking for her, I drove it to her—to out in front of her house and walked back downtown. Only took ten minutes or so."

"So you and Amber saw it on your way home," I say.

She nods.

"Amber falls asleep and you go back for the car," I say. "You . . . you had worked on a sex trafficking project in school. Knew one of those hotels or brothels would be the perfect place to dump her body. You reached out to Natasha Phillips to do a podcast about Qwon's case, told her you knew of her because of the reporting she had done on sex trafficking in Florida. So you drove to Jacksonville with her body in the trunk. Did you take your mom's cellphone? Angel's? Will the records show pings to them from your trip? You then took off all her clothes and everything that would identify her. You left the necklace that had been her grandmother's but you took off the ring Qwon had given her. That stood out to me. Did you stage it to look like she had been sexually assaulted there or had you already done that?"

The group expresses various forms of verbal and nonverbal revulsion and takes another slight step back, away from her.

She shakes her head and begins to cry. "I . . . she . . . she was already dead. I wouldn't have done anything to . . . I just wanted it to look like she was . . . by a guy."

"How'd you do it?" I ask. "Where?"

She shakes her head again. "I can't. I . . ."

"You certainly fuckin' can," Buck says. "Tell us. If you can do that sick fuckin' shit to my little girl you can goddamn sure tell us. NOW."

"I . . . a condom on the end of a . . . of the . . . tire iron I found in the trunk."

Kay begins to sob.

Buck grabs a chair and hurls it across the courtyard.

"I'm so sorry," Kathryn says. "It was just to make it look like . . . I . . . I'm so—"

"Don't you fuckin' say you're sorry again," Buck says. "Don't you fuckin' dare. I'll kill you if you do. I swear. I swear to Christ I will."

She almost apologizes to him, but catches herself.

"Then you drove home, parked the car at the airport, walked or hitchhiked home. Amber thought you left before she woke up because you got a call about Angel being missing, but you hadn't been there all night."

"How could you?" Qwon says.

"I . . . love you. Always have."

I recall her singing *I Will Always Love You* the night we went out to the Saltshaker Lounge, all the raw emotion she expressed, her tears, and I now know why—now know who she was singing it to.

"You let me sit in prison for eighteen years," he says, shaking his head, seeming unable to understand. "*Eighteen years.*"

"I . . . I never intended to. I kept thinking I could get you out and stay out myself so we could be together. I tried everything. I knew I could get you out and I did. Finally."

Qwon continues to shake his head, seeming incapable of processing any of this like everyone else gathered here.

"I'm so sorry," Justice says, shaking his head. "I had no idea. They told me you did it."

"I understand," Qwon says. "I do. I got no . . . Half my life's over. Got no time for hate or grudges."

"I took money," he says. "The Crime Stoppers reward. I'm . . . I feel so ashamed. I'll pay back every cent. I'll make it right. I'll do whatever I can to make sure you have the best life possible. I swear it."

Kathryn looks at her parents, at Ida, at her classmates. "Please forgive me. I didn't mean to. I'm . . . so . . . for what I did. I honestly am."

"You could've confessed years ago," Kay says. "Could've let us know where our daughter's body was. They cremated her and scattered her ashes in the Atlantic. We didn't get to . . . she was alone all that time. She was put to rest as a Jane Doe. No. You could've done something years go. You didn't. Buck's right. Don't act like you're sorry now. Don't ask for our forgiveness now just because you got caught. Don't you dare."

"She's right, child," Ida says. "You could've ended Qwon's suffering. Theirs. You did nothing."

"I did everything I could to free—to get Qwon out. Hell, I helped John solve the case. Ask him? I've always been so torn. I helped him find out what happened to the body. I—"

"Only while trying to save your own skin."

"No. That's what I'm saying. I wanted to make it right. I did. I tried. And eventually I . . . have. I'm . . . everyone knows now and I helped make that happen. But what happened to Angel was just an accident."

Billy says, "I think somebody needs to explain to your ass what the definition of *accident* is."

"It was no accident," Ida says.

"I mean I didn't mean to do it. I just snapped. I would never do something like that. Not ever. I know because I never did anything like that before and I've never done anything like that since. But since there was nothing I could do for her at that point . . ."

"Say her name, goddamnit," Buck yells. "Don't just say *her*. You murdered Angel. My Angel."

"*Angel*," Kathryn says, "I couldn't do anything for Angel, but . . . I could try to do something for Qwon and me. And I tried. I tried so hard. Time just passed by and before I knew it, eighteen years had passed. I didn't marry. I didn't have kids. I really didn't have a life. I just worked on freeing the man I love. I'm sorry. God, I'm so sorry. I wish I could take it back. I wish I could undo . . . what happened. Don't you think I would if I could?"

"You could've done so much more than you did," Kay says.

Buck looks at Henry and Mary Elizabeth. "We stood up for Qwon," he says. "Stood by y'all all this time and . . . your . . . kid . . . killed mine. Murdered her. After . . . committing incest. My Angel did nothing wrong. *Nothing*. She just walked up on . . ."

"We had no idea," Henry says. "We would've done something if we did. You know we would."

"What you could've done was not raise an evil, murderous bitch."

"I'm not evil," Kathryn says. "I'm not murderous. I snapped and in an instant I committed one terrible, horrible act."

"*One?*" Billy says. "*One?* I think somebody needs to explain to your ass what the definition of *one* is."

I know how long it takes to strangle someone and it's far more than an instant. She had ample opportunity to stop, to gather herself and undo what she was doing before the point at which it couldn't be undone. And she didn't.

Pinter steps over to Kathryn and begins cuffing her.

"No," Mary Elizabeth says. "Not my . . . We just got Qwon back. Don't take our—"

"It's okay, Mom," Kathryn says. "It's what I deserve. I'm sorry. I never meant for any of this to happen. I really didn't. Please know that. Please know I'm not a bad person. I just lost it once in a drug-addled state. Mr and Mrs. Diaz and . . . Qwon . . . I've caused you so much pain, done you the most wrong. I . . . I don't have any more words. Just . . . I'm so . . . I truly, truly am."

Pinter leads her out.

For a long beat no one says anything, just stands there in stunned, drained silence, the only sounds soft cries and sniffles.

Eventually, slowly, wordlessly people begin to drift out of the courtyard, onto the sidewalk, and disappear into the night.

I check on Ida, Qwon, the Diazes, and thank Merrill and Za again.

Then Anna takes my hand and takes me home.

Chapter Forty-seven

"You okay?" Anna asks.

We're on Highway 22 heading home. The night is dark and a low fog hovers over the highway. It has been several miles since we passed a car and our headlights are diffused and ineffectual.

I nod.

"You sure?"

"Yeah. Takes a toll. Wouldn't have chosen any of it. But . . . knew when I signed up for this work there were no happy endings."

She starts to say something, but I interrupt her.

"Except," I add, "we're going home together."

"Doesn't get any happier ending than that," she says. "That and we get Johanna tomorrow. We'll all be together this weekend."

"Wasn't long ago I'd get to the end of a case and didn't have that."

"Has Susan said when she's moving down here?"

"Plans to look for a place this weekend," I say. "Heading over there after she drops Johanna off."

"So you don't have to drive to Atlanta and back?"

"I do not."

"Oh, that's just . . . the best news. I want you to sleep in and spend the day relaxing and resting when you're not making love to me."

"You got it."

"Thought any more about resigning one of your jobs?" she asks.

I shake my head. "That one's in the suspension folder for now. Gonna give it a little more time before I do anything."

"You sure you're okay? I was worried about how you might be feeling about Ida, about how this affects her," she says. "Given how it . . . ended, who it was. I didn't want you feeling even guiltier than you did before you agreed to help her again."

"I'm . . . it was so different this time. And she made sure I didn't feel any . . . I'm good. We're good."

"Good," she says, pausing before adding, "I'm so proud of you. So honored to be sharing this life with you. I love the way your mind works, love watching you work, the way you piece things together, make connections no one does."

"You and Merrill did as much as I did," I say. "More. And if either of you had had all the various pieces you could've put it together."

"No, that's not true. We couldn't. But that's beside the point. The point is . . . I'm in awe of you and I will never, ever take you—the gift of you—for granted."

"Thank you."

"I think I like your mind second only to your kindness," she says. "I don't know. Maybe it's your kindness, your spirit or essence, then your mind. I'll have to think about it."

I smile. "You're trying to cheer me up," I say. "You're the best wife in the whole wide world. But I really am fine."

"I may or may not be trying to cheer you up, but I meant every word I said."

When we pull into our driveway, Chris Taunton is there in our yard. Dad is near him, gun drawn.

"I want you to go straight inside and check on Taylor, Sam, and Verna, okay?" I say.

"Okay."

"Don't even look at him."

"Don't worry."

I pull onto the grass close to the door, placing the car so that it blocks Anna completely as she gets out and walks in.

"Let me get out first," I say. "Give me five seconds, then you go. Take the keys in case Dad locked the door. He probably did."

I slip the little .38 out of my ankle holster, pat Anna's hand, tell her I love her, and get out of the car, gun drawn.

"Dad," I say. "You okay?"

"Damn, what's with all the guns?" Chris says. "This how you rednecks greet every newcomer to town?"

"I'm good," Dad says. "Was just trying to explain to Chris here how it's not a good idea to just drop by."

I look at Chris. "Don't just not drop by, don't ever come here again. Not ever."

"John, my family lives here. My flesh and blood. She's my daughter, not yours. You think you're gonna keep me from my daughter? You really think that?"

"You're wrong, Chris. Your family doesn't live here. Mine does. If the court grants you supervised visitation we'll deal with that, but it won't be here. Don't ever come here."

"No one's gonna keep me from my family," he says. "No one. Not you, not the courts. No one. I will be visiting my daughter. And I will be doing it any goddamn time I feel like it."

"You know," I say, "until this moment I thought the Stand Your Ground law was mostly a joke—used by the paranoid and mentally ill to shoot people in movie theaters and gas stations—but now . . . . I'm seeing other more legitimate and necessary applications."

"What're you saying *Chaplain* John?" he says in an exaggerated, mocking manner.

"I'll speak slowly," I say, "and not use any figurative language or subtlety. You are trespassing. I've told you to leave and not to ever come back. You tried to kill us. Not just me and Anna, but your own child."

He shakes his head. "I was only tryin' to kill you."

"You represent a very real threat to my family. If you come back on my property again, I will shoot you."

Dad shakes his head. "No you won't, Son. And he knows it. You won't get the chance, 'cause I'll shoot his sorry ass first."

"I'll say goodnight now," Chris says, his voice and demeanor calm, casual, "but I'll see y'all again real soon. Y'all might not see me, but I'll see you. I'll see you."

"We know you're a coward and a back shooter," I say, "someone who hires others to do his dirty deeds, but know this—if you do anything or have anything done to any of us, we have friends who will square it."

"And be damn happy to do so," Dad says.

"Anything happens to any of us, they're coming after you," I say. "So you better pray nothing happens. Nothing at all."

He turns and walks away. "Night," he says, lifting a hand back toward us. "See you soon."

He slowly, nonchalantly, walks down our driveway and then our street, and disappears into the night in front of the old Wewa Hardware building.

Dad turns to me and says, "He's gonna be a problem until he's put down."

I nod. "I know," I say. "I know."

Later that night, as I lie awake thinking about what to do about Chris, my weapon on the bedside table next to me, my phone begins to vibrate.

"Congratulations," Randa says. "I really thought it was the other ex. But like you said . . . I was guessing. Tryin' to get ahead of you on it. But . . . anyway . . . Good work."

"When can we expect Daniel?" I ask. "Can I come get him now?"

"You won, John," she says. "You did. *Mr. Big Brain*. But the truth is all that really does is tie us up. It's even now—one-one. But I'm not one to not settle a score."

"Oh, I know this about you," I say.

She actually laughs. "Sorry about the mess I left you in Eastpoint, but no, I meant I pay my debts . . . I understand that murdering piece of shit ex-husband of Anna's is getting out of prison, that the charges against him are being dropped. So here's what I'm gonna do . . . I'm gonna take him off the board for you. Punch his ticket. Cancel him to cancel my debt and then we'll play again someday soon for Daniel. How's that?"

But before I can tell her that's not okay, not to do anything to Chris, she is gone and I'm left alone again with my thoughts and possibilities and options—which all just got a lot more complicated.

About the Author

Michael grew up in North Florida near the Gulf of Mexico and the Apalachicola River in a small town world famous for tupelo honey.

Truly a regional writer, North Florida is his beat.

Captivated by story since childhood, Michael has a love for language and narrative inspired by the Southern storytelling tradition that captured his imagination and became such a source of meaning and inspiration. He holds undergraduate and graduate degrees in theology with an emphasis on myth and narrative.

In the early 90s, Michael became the youngest chaplain within the Florida Department of Corrections. For nearly a decade, he served as a contract, staff, then senior chaplain at three different facilities in the Panhandle of Florida—a unique experience that led to his first novel, 1997's critically acclaimed, **POWER IN THE BLOOD**. Michael's books take readers through the electronically locked gates of the chain-link fences, beneath the looping razor wire glinting in the sun, and into the strange world of Potter Correctional Institution, Florida's toughest maximum security prison.

Michael lives with his wife Dawn in Wewa-hitchka, FL.

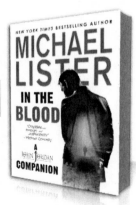